Arabel and Mortimer

JOAN AIKEN

Arabel and Mortimer

Illustrated by
Quentin Blake

An Odyssey Classic
Harcourt, Inc.
Orlando Austin New York San Diego London

www.HarcourtBooks.com

First published by Doubleday & Company, Inc., New York, 1981
First Odyssey Classics edition 2007

Library of Congress Cataloging-in-Publication Data
Aiken, Joan, 1924–2004.
Arabel and Mortimer/Joan Aiken; illustrated by Quentin Blake.
v.   cm.
Summary: Presents three previously published works
about a pet raven named Mortimer, who talks, eats everything
in sight, and causes all sorts of trouble.
Contents: Mortimer's tie—The spiral stair—Mortimer and
the sword Excalibur. [1. Ravens—Fiction. 2. Birds as pets—Fiction.
3. Humorous stories.] I. Blake, Quentin, ill. II. Title.
PZ7.A2695Ap   2007
[Fic]—dc22   2006102554
ISBN 978-0-15-206082-4

Text set in Bodoni
Designed by Cathy Riggs

A C E G H F D B

Printed in the United States of America

Contents

Mortimer's Tie

1

On a beautiful sunny, warm Saturday halfway through March, something happened in Rainwater Crescent which was to lead to such startling consequences for the Jones family that even years afterward Mrs. Jones was liable to get lightheaded if she so much as heard a piano being played—while the sight of a tin of lavender paint, or any object that had been painted a lavender color, brought her out in severe palpitations. As for Mr. Jones, he was often heard to declare that he would let mushrooms grow on the floor of his taxi—or even mustard and cress—before he would permit any person other than himself to clean it out ever again.

Perhaps it will be best to start at the beginning.

On Saturday afternoons Mr. Jones, who was a taxi driver, always allowed himself two hours off to watch football. (In winter, that is, of course; in summer he watched cricket.) If the Rumbury Wanderers were playing on their home ground—which was just five minutes' walk from the Jones family house in Rainwater Crescent, Rumbury Town, London N.W. 3½— Mr. Jones went round to cheer his home team; otherwise he looked at whatever game was being shown on television.

On the Saturday in question he had just returned from a special hire job, taking a passenger to Rumbury Docks. He was back late, so he bolted down his lunch and went off to watch Rumbury play Camden Town.

Mrs. Jones was out doing her usual Saturday shopping and having her hair set at Norma's Ninth Wave; otherwise things might have turned out differently.

While Mr. Jones was taking his time off, Chris Cross, who had just done his A levels at Rumbury Comprehensive, cleaned out Mr. Jones's taxi, which was left parked for the purpose in front of the house in Rainwater Crescent.

For doing this job Chris got paid one pound plus an extra good high tea. Arabel Jones, who was still too young for school, helped Chris, but she did it for pleasure and did not get paid; however, she got a

share of the high tea and had free rides all the time in her father's taxi, so the arrangement seemed fair.

Mortimer, the Jones family raven, also helped clean the cab; or at least he was present while the job was being done.

The way Chris set about it was as follows: first he carried Mrs. Jones's vacuum cleaner (it was the upright kind and was called a Baby Vampire) out onto the pavement in front of the house, taking its cord through the drawing-room window and across the garden (luckily it was a good long cord); Chris then removed the rubber mats from the floor of the taxi, laid them on the pavement, and washed them; then he vacuumed the inside of the taxi with the Baby Vampire; then he washed the floor with hot water and Swoosh detergent.

Next, using the garden hose, he washed the outside of the taxi all over (first making sure the windows were shut). Then he gave the windows and windshield an extra going over with Windazz. Then he gave the rest of the outside a polish. Then he put back the floor mats, which had had time to dry by now, and cleaned the inside upholstery with Seatsope. He finished off by polishing the door and window handles and any other shiny bits on the dashboard with Chromoshino.

Or at least that was all that Chris intended to do. But Mortimer the raven was taking such an active interest in the proceedings that matters turned out differently.

First Mortimer sat on the vacuum cleaner and had all his tail feathers blown sideways. Also a green tie, which he happened to be wearing, wound several times round his neck, became unwound, and was blown twenty-five yards down the street. Arabel had to go after it; she rolled it up and put it into the glove compartment for safekeeping. Mortimer, slightly irritated by having his tail disarranged, had in the meantime pecked a hole in the bag of the vacuum cleaner, so Chris had to do the rest of the job with the brush and dustpan.

Then Mortimer got tangled up in the hose. During his frantic efforts to disentangle himself he pecked several holes in the hosepipe; after that, water came out all over the place.

Next, Mortimer trod on the cake of Seatsope which Chris had carelessly left on the front doorstep; it skidded away with Mortimer on it and narrowly missed a passing mail van. So Arabel decided it might be better to move Mortimer inside the taxi.

Here he perched on the rim of the pail containing hot water and Swoosh. There was not much water left in the pail, which tipped over with Mortimer's weight. Mortimer swiftly removed himself from the floor, where he had been ankle-deep in Swoosh suds, and clambered onto the steering wheel, where he studied all the dashboard fittings with keen attention.

"It would be a lot easier to get on with the job if that bird stayed indoors," said Chris, wringing out the bottoms of his jeans and giving Mortimer an unfriendly look. Both Arabel and Chris were wet all over by this time, what with one thing and another, while Mortimer was perfectly dry; the water just ran off his thick black feathers.

"Ma doesn't like Mortimer to be left alone indoors," Arabel said, "not after the time he ate all the taps off the gas cooker. He didn't *mean* to knock over the bucket. Why don't you switch on the heater? That will dry the floor."

Chris had the car keys in his jeans pocket. He moved Mortimer off the steering wheel and onto the backseat; then he stuck the key in and turned on the ignition; then he switched on the fan heater, which began to blow hot air all over the place.

Mortimer had been watching all this with absorbed interest. He had been thinking a lot about keys lately; in fact, he had started a small collection of them which he kept in an old money box of Arabel's at the back of the broom cupboard.

Now Mortimer stepped thoughtfully down onto the floor (leaving some toenail holes in the leather upholstery) and began to walk about, enjoying the warm draft on his stomach; he also left dirty bird footprints on the damp floor.

"I wish he'd keep his feet in his pockets," said Chris.

"He hasn't any pockets," said Arabel.

Mortimer then returned to the steering wheel in three quick movements—flap, hop, thump—and tweaked out the ignition key with his strong, hairy beak. Next he flopped right out of the taxi through the open front door and made his way quite fast to the letter box which stood on the pavement outside the Jones house. He was just at the point of dropping the car keys through the slot of the letter box when Chris, leaping from the taxi like a grasshopper, grabbed him around the middle and took back the keys.

"*No* you don't, buster; you just keep your big beak out of what doesn't concern you," said Chris; he dumped Mortimer none too gently on the rear seat once more.

Mortimer began to sulk. The way he did this was to sink his head between his shoulders, ruffle up his neck feathers, turn his beak sideways, curl up his

claws, and, in general, look as if for two pins he would puncture the tires or smash the windows.

"He wants to help, *really*," said Arabel. "The trouble is, he doesn't know how. Tell you what, Mortimer. Why don't you hunt for diamonds behind the backseat?"

Mortimer gave Arabel a very sour look. Actually, until a few days ago he had been quite keen on searching for diamonds; it had been his favorite hobby and he did it all over the place, but specially under carpets, in garbage bins, coal scuttles, and paper-and-string drawers; but he had found so few diamonds—indeed, none—that he had lately lost interest in this pastime. Instead, he had become interested in keys. He liked the way they fitted into locks and the different things that happened when the keys were turned—like engines starting and doors opening.

He had developed an interest in letter boxes, too.

So he was not pleased at being asked to hunt for diamonds.

However, when Arabel pointed out to him the deep crack between the cushion and the back of the rear seat, he began to poke along it in a grudging manner, as if he were doing her a big favor.

In fact, the crack *was* very narrow and inviting, just the right place to find a diamond, and his beak was just the right length to go into it nicely.

The surprising thing was that almost at once Mortimer did find a diamond, quite a big one, the size of a stewed prune. It was set in a platinum ring.

"Kaaaark!" said Mortimer, very amazed.

The remark came out slightly muffled, as if Mortimer had a cold, because the platinum ring was jammed over his beak.

"Oh!" said Arabel. "Chris! Just *look* what Mortimer's found!"

She slid the ring off Mortimer's beak just in time, for otherwise he would almost certainly have scraped it off with his claw and then swallowed it.

"Coo," said Chris. "What a size! That stone is probably worth half Rumbury Town. D'you think we ought to fetch your dad?"

"Pa simply hates to come home before the match is finished," said Arabel.

Just at that moment they heard the phone inside the house begin to ring. Arabel went in through the open front door to answer it, slipping the ring on her finger.

Mortimer sidled after her, keeping a sharp eye on the ring. But as he passed the front door he poked a worm, which he had picked up for the purpose, through the letter slot into the basket behind.

The Joneses' telephone stood on the windowsill halfway up the stairs.

"Hullo?" said Arabel, picking up the receiver and sitting on the middle step.

"Hullo?" said a lady's voice. "Oh my goodness can I speak to Mr. Jones the taxi driver who drove me to Rumbury Docks this morning? This is Lady Dunnage speaking. Mr. Jones took me to launch my hubby's new cruise liner the *Queen of Bethnal Green*—"

All these words came out very fast and breathless, joined together like the ribbon of paper from a cash register.

"I'm afraid Mr. Jones is out just now watching football," said Arabel. "This is his daughter speaking."

"Oh my goodness then dear when will your father be back? The thing is, I've lost my diamond ring which is worth two hundred and seventy thousand, four hundred and twenty-two pounds—I just looked

down at my finger and it wasn't there the ring I mean the finger is there of course—and my hubby will be upset when he finds out—specially if it fell into Rumbury Dock—I just wondered if it could have come off in the taxi when I took my gloves off to unwrap a lemon throat lozenge—"

"Oh, yes, that's quite all right, we found it," said Arabel. "The ring, I mean."

"You *have*? You really have? Oh, what a relief! Oh, goodness, I feel quite trembly. I'll come round at once and fetch it as soon as I can get back—I'm in Bishop's Stortford now, opening a multistory amusement park—"

"Kaaaark," said Mortimer, who was now sitting on Arabel's shoulder listening to this conversation.

"I beg your pardon, dear?"

"Oh, that was our raven, Mortimer. It was Mortimer who found your ring, actually," said Arabel.

"Really? Fancy," said Lady Dunnage. "I've got a parrot called Isabella and she's ever so clever at finding things. Well, I can tell you, there will be a handsome reward for *everyone* concerned in finding my ring, and please, please don't let it out of your sight till I get there."

"That was Lady Dunnage, the person who owns the ring," said Arabel, returning to Chris. He had taken advantage of Mortimer's absence to replace the mats and clean up the upholstery. "She's going to call in and pick up the ring as soon as she can get back from Bishop's Stortford, so we shan't need to fetch Pa from the football match."

"How do you know it was her and not a gang of international jewel thieves?" said Chris.

"I didn't think of that," said Arabel. "Do you think we ought to tell the police about it?"

She looked at the huge diamond on her finger, which Mortimer was eyeing, too. However, at this moment Mrs. Jones came up the street with a basket full of shopping and a carton of banana-nut-raisin ice cream under her arm, and her hair all smooth and curly and tinted Bohemian brown, which is the color of the gritty kind of instant coffee, but a lot shinier.

As soon as she caught sight of the large flashing stone on Arabel's finger, Mrs. Jones began to scold.

"How often have I told you not to go to Woolworth's without me, Arabel Jones, you naughty girl, there's mumps about and I told you to stay right here at home till I got back and not leave Mortimer liable to get up to mischief I declare as soon as I leave the house trouble sets in and spending your pocket money on that trashy Woolworth's jewelry instead of a nice sensible toy or even a book—"

"It's all right, Ma," said Arabel. "I didn't get the ring at Woolworth's. Mortimer found it in Pa's taxi and the lady it belongs to, Lady Dunnage, is coming round to fetch it as soon as she can—"

"Lady *Dunnage?*" screeched Mrs. Jones. "And me with the best cushion covers at the laundry, no tea ready, a week's shopping to put away, soapy water all over the front steps, and the hose and the Baby Vampire and goodness knows what else out on the pavement—"

However, they all helped put these things away, as well as the bucket, the sponge, the soap, the brush and dustpan, the various rags and bits of towel and tins of cleaner and polish and Windazz and Seatsope and Chromoshino that Chris had been using.

Even Mortimer carried in the cake of Seatsope, but as he was later found to have dropped it into the kettle, his help was not greatly valued; he sat on the kitchen taps looking melancholy, with one foot on the cold, one foot on the hot, and his tail dangling into the sink, while

Mrs. Jones emptied out the kettleful of hot froth and put on some more water to boil in a saucepan.

By the time Lady Dunnage arrived they had tea set out on the table with three kinds of cake, sausages and chips and eggs, sardine salad, a plateful of meringues, a plateful of Kreemy Kokonut Surprises, and masses of biscuits.

Even Mortimer cheered up; although he still felt unappreciated, he loved sausages and chips and meringues. If allowed, he speared the sausages with his beak, threw the chips into the air before swallowing them, and jumped on the meringues till they collapsed. He had not come across Kreemy Kokonut Surprises before, but they looked to him just the right size to stuff down the sink waste pipe.

When Lady Dunnage finally arrived, she did not seem in the least like a member of a gang of international jewel thieves. She was quite short, all dressed in furs, and her hair was just as shiny and curly as Mrs. Jones's, but the color of a lemon sponge. As soon as she was inside the door she cried out:

"Oh, I can see you are all just as good and kind as you can be and just like dear Mr. Jones who is my favorite taxi driver and I always ask for him when I ring up the cab stand and I'm so grateful I hardly know what to say words fail me they really do for I should never have heard the last of it from my husband Sir Horatio Dunnage if that ring had been lost it was my engagement ring that he bought for me twenty years ago last January and which would you rather have two thousand pounds or a cruise to Spain on the *Queen of Bethnal Green*?"

"I beg your pardon, dear?" said Mrs. Jones, quite puzzled, pouring the guest a cup of tea.

"The *Queen of Bethnal Green*, that's my husband's new cruise liner. He's Sir Horatio Dunnage, you know, who owns the Star Line and the Garter Line and now this new Brace and Tackle line, so say the word and you can all come for a ten-day cruise in a first-class suite sailing on Saturday the nineteenth. Now which would you really rather have, that or the two thousand pounds?"

2

Ooo—I've *always* wanted to go on a cruise!"
Mrs. Jones could hardly believe her luck.
But then she remembered something and
said, "Really, it was Mortimer who found the ring,
though, wasn't it, Arabel dearie? I don't know if he'd
like a cruise, what do you think?"

"I expect he would," said Arabel. "He generally
likes new things. Would you like a cruise, do you
think, Mortimer?"

Mortimer thought he would. He couldn't reply, for
his beak was full of Kreemy Kokonut Surprise, but
his eyes sparkled and he began to jump up and down
on the back of Arabel's chair.

"Of course he'd like it, bless him!" said Lady Dunnage. "My parrot, Isabella, just loves being on board ships. That's settled, then! I'll get my hubby's secretary to send you a note about embarkation time. I'll be on the cruise myself, as it's the first one, and so will Isabella, and I'm sure she and Mortimer will make great friends."

"I don't know if Mortimer's ever met a parrot," said Arabel a little doubtfully. "But I expect it will be all right."

Arabel herself was greatly excited at the thought of a cruise. But Chris, when Lady Dunnage invited him, said he always got seasick in boats, and he would really prefer a little cash to put toward a motorbike for which he was saving up. Lady Dunnage promised that he should have not the money but the bike itself the very next day. Then she left them, gazing so happily at her recovered ring that she never even noticed the worm in the letter box on the back of the front door.

When Mr. Jones came home after the football match and heard from his enthusiastic family that they were all going on a cruise to Spain, which they had chosen instead of two thousand pounds, he was very put out indeed.

"Going on a *cruise*? To *Spain*? In *March*? Taking *Mortimer*? Instead of two thousand hard cash? You must be stark, staring barmy," he said. "Mark my words, no good will come of this."

He was really annoyed. He threw down his evening paper and a Rumbury Wanderers football scarf and went off to watch television, calling back over his shoulder, "Anyway, what's that child doing up so late? It's high time she *and* that bird were in bed. Cruise to Spain, indeed. What next, I should like to know?"

After Arabel and Mortimer had gone slowly upstairs, Arabel remembered that Mortimer's green tie had been left outside in the glove compartment of her father's taxi; she had to put on her trousers and duffle coat over her pajamas and go down again to

get it. Mortimer would not have dreamed of going to bed without his green tie.

So, on the Saturday following Mortimer's discovery of Lady Dunnage's diamond ring, the Jones family set off on their cruise to Spain.

To start with, Mr. Jones's friend, Mr. Murphy, drove them in his taxi to Rumbury Docks. Rain was coming down as if someone had tipped it out of a pail, and when they got out of the taxi an east wind as sharp as a bread knife came slicing along the dock to meet them.

Mortimer was in a bad mood. At that moment he would much rather have been peacefully at home, asleep in the bread bin, with his green tie wrapped round and round his neck and his head tucked under his wing, and perhaps a bunch of keys hooked over one of his toenails.

However, when he saw the cruise liner on which they were to set sail, he began to take more interest in the adventure.

The *Queen of Bethnal Green* was all painted white and blue and sparkling with newness. She had three white spikes sticking up from her top, four rows of portholes, and a very large blue-and-white-striped funnel, or smokestack.

A friendly steward was waiting by the gangway to escort the Jones family to their quarters. By now

Mortimer had become so interested in everything around him that he wanted to walk up the gangway backward, very slowly, but it was raining too hard for that; Arabel picked him up and carried him on board.

Their cabins were up on the top deck, so they went up in a lift, together with their luggage. Mr. and Mrs. Jones were in a large room with two beds and several armchairs. Arabel and Mortimer were next door; their cabin was smaller but much nicer, for it had bunks with pink blankets, one above the other, instead of mere beds.

Arabel would have preferred the upper bunk (which was reached by a ladder), but Mortimer climbed into it directly, going up the ladder beak over claw, very fast, and made it quite plain that he was not going to stand for any arguments about their sleeping arrangements.

"We'll be lucky if he hasn't eaten the ladder before the end of the trip," Mr. Jones said, "seeing how he nibbles the stairs at home."

"Nevermore," said Mortimer.

Mr. Jones looked out at the rain, which was splashing down onto the deck outside the porthole.

"I'm sure I don't know how you're ever going to keep that bird occupied and out of mischief for ten days, not if the weather's like this all the way. Have you brought anything for him to do?"

"He's got his tie," said Arabel.

The tie was an old green one that had once belonged to Mr. Jones. Just before Christmas Mortimer had found it in a ragbag and had taken a fancy to it. When he was feeling tired, or bad-tempered, or sulky, or sad, or just thoughtful, he liked to wind the tie round his neck (which he did by taking one end in his beak and then slowly and deliberately turning round and round); when the tie was all wound up, he

would proceed to work his head and beak (still holding the other end of the tie) well in under his left wing, and he would then sit like that for a long time. One rather inconvenient feature of this habit was that Mortimer preferred the tie to be ice cold when he put it on; if, when he suddenly felt the need for the tie, he found that it had been left lying in the sun or near the fire, and felt warm to the touch, he was quite likely to fly into a passion, croaking and flapping and jumping up and down and shouting "Nevermore" at the top of his lungs.

On account of this, when they were at home, in spite of Mrs. Jones's grumbles, Arabel kept the tie in the ice compartment of the refrigerator so that it was always nice and cold, ready for use. And if they were going on a trip somewhere, in Mr. Jones's taxi or in a train, Arabel trailed the tie out of the window, holding tightly to one end. There had been an awkward occasion once when it got wrapped around a motorbike policeman's helmet. But that is another story.

Arabel began to worry now about the temperature of the tie. Her cabin was centrally heated—very warm—and the portholes were not the kind that opened.

"Do you think there is a fridge on this ship where we could keep the tie?" she asked her father.

"I'll see to it for you," said the steward, who was just carrying in Arabel's suitcase. "The lady in the next cabin has a big suite with a kitchenette; I'll put it in her fridge. Then, anytime you want it, ring for me—press that red button there over your dressing table—and I'll come along and get it out for you. My name's Mike."

"Won't the lady mind?" said Arabel.

"Not her. It's Miss Brandy Brown, the lady who's in charge of entertainment on the ship; her and that group they call the Stepney Stepalives. She's hardly ever in her cabin."

Arabel and Mortimer followed Mike into the corridor and watched him unlock the door next to theirs, tuck the tie into Miss Brandy Brown's refrigerator, and then, after he had locked up again, put the bunch of keys he carried back into the pocket of his white jacket.

"You'll be all right, then," said Mr. Jones. "After we've unpacked, we'll all go along for a cup of tea," and he went back to his and Mrs. Jones's cabin.

Arabel and Mortimer took stock of their new

quarters. As well as the pink-blanketed bunks, they had a desk and a dressing table, two armchairs, and a whole lot of mirrors; Mortimer discovered that by looking into one mirror which faced another, he could see an endless procession of reflected black ravens going off into the distance, which he enjoyed very much indeed.

There was also a large cupboard for their clothes, and a bathroom.

When Mortimer discovered the bathroom he became even more enthusiastic, because it had a shower, and he had never come across one before. He spent about twenty minutes pressing all the knobs and getting terrific spouts of hot and cold water. After three inches of water had accumulated on the bathroom floor, Arabel began to be afraid that the water might slop over the doorsill into the bedroom.

"I think you'd better come out now, Mortimer," she said.

Mortimer took no notice.

But then Arabel, happening to glance out of the porthole, saw Rumbury Docks sliding past at a very rapid rate.

"Oh, look, quick, Mortimer!" she said. "We're moving! We're going down the Thames!"

In fact, now that they thought about it, they could feel the boat bouncing a little through the water, and just then the siren gave a tremendously loud blast:

Woooooooooooop. Mortimer nearly jumped out of his feathers at the noise. And when Arabel held him up to look out through the porthole and see all the London docks rushing past, he wasn't as pleased as she had expected him to be; he suddenly looked rather unhappy, as if his breakfast had disagreed with him.

"My goodness, we're going fast already; we're simply shooting along," said Arabel.

"Nevermore," muttered Mortimer gloomily.

Not long after this, Mr. and Mrs. Jones put their heads round the door to say that they were going along to the Rumpus Lounge for tea and entertainment by Miss Brandy Brown.

"Come on, Mortimer," said Arabel. "I'm sure you'll enjoy that."

She picked up Mortimer, hugging him tightly, and followed her parents down the long corridor.

The Rumpus Lounge was a huge room, all decorated in brown and pink and gold, with a balcony round it. On the balcony, and underneath it, were small tables and chairs. In the middle of the room was a big bare space where people were dancing. There was also a grand piano at one side.

Outside the windows, the banks of the river Thames were getting farther and farther away; in fact, they were almost out of sight, and the *Queen of Bethnal Green* was rolling and bouncing up and down a good deal more as she moved into the open sea.

The Jones family sat down at one of the little tables beside the dance floor and a waiter brought them tea and cakes. Mortimer began to look more cheerful.

A small and very lively lady walked over to the piano. She had hair the color of a rusty chrysanthemum and pink cheeks and flashing eyes and a dress that was absolutely covered with sequins which looked like brand-new tenpenny pieces.

She began to play the piano and sing a song at the same time.

> *"Swinging down to Spain*
> *Never mind the rain,*
> *Way, hay, yodelay,*
> *What a happy holiday*
> *Just wait till you tell them where you've been*
> *On the* Queen of Bethnal Green!"

Unfortunately, Mortimer soon began to get over-excited while this was going on and to shout, "Nevermore! *Nevermore!*" at the end of each verse and sometimes in the middle as well; the lady began to cast some very annoyed glances in their direction, and presently a waiter came to ask if they could please keep their bird a little quieter, as Miss Brandy Brown didn't like being interrupted.

She started singing another song.

"Sail bonny boat like a bird in the air
Over the sea to Spain
Oh what a riot of fun we'll share
Out on the bounding main
Dancing and singing and eating and
    drinking
Cancel all care and pain
If we were clever we'd sail on and never
Ever go home again..."

Mortimer seemed to disagree strongly with the sentiment of this song, for he muttered, "Never, never, never, never, never, never, KAAARK," all the time that Miss Brown was singing it, his voice growing louder and louder, until she suddenly lost patience, left the piano, and strode over to their table.

Keeping their large silver teapot warm was a blue quilted tea cozy; Miss Brown picked this up and clapped it over Mortimer like a fire extinguisher. Then she walked away; just in time, as Mortimer kicked off the tea cozy in about five seconds flat and emerged looking very indignant indeed.

Luckily, at this moment Lady Dunnage appeared and came up to their table; she was wearing a pink-and-gray silk dress and she carried, perched on a bracelet on her wrist, a gray parrot with a long scarlet tail. Mortimer's eyes almost shot out on stalks when he saw the parrot; he became completely silent and stared with all his might. The parrot stared back. She had a beak that was curved like the back of a spoon, and she looked very knowing indeed.

"I do hope you are enjoying yourselves, dears," said Lady Dunnage.

"Oh yes, thank you, dear, we're having ever such a nice time," said Mrs. Jones.

"This is my parrot, Isabella," said Lady Dunnage.

"Kaaaark," said Mortimer.

"I've arranged for you to sit at Captain Mainbrace's table for dinner; he has a son called Henry who is about your age, Arabel. And do let me know if there's anything you want in the meantime."

"Oh please," said Arabel, "could your parrot come to my cabin and play with Mortimer? I think he'd like that."

"Certainly," said Lady Dunnage graciously. "I'm sure Isabella would enjoy it, too. When she wants to

come back to me, just let her out into the passage; she knows her way all over this ship, as we came on board such a lot while it was being built."

"Can she talk?" Arabel asked.

"Not really yet; she's only a year old. All she can say is 'hard cheese.'"

Arabel went back to her cabin with a bird perched on each shoulder. In spite of the very good tea, she knew that Mortimer had not been enjoying himself in the Rumpus Lounge; somehow his bright black eyes didn't seem as bright as usual, and he kept swallowing; Arabel was worried in case he wasn't going to be happy on the cruise.

However, once back in the cabin he seemed to cheer up. Arabel had thought the two birds might like to play with marbles or tiddledywinks, both of which she had brought with her, but they did not; they took turns climbing the ladder to the upper bunk and then jumping off on top of each other.

Then they took turns shutting each other in Arabel's suitcase and bursting out with a loud shriek. Then they had a very enjoyable fight, rolling all over the floor and kicking each other; showers of red, gray, and black feathers flew about. Mortimer shouted, "Nevermore!" and Isabella screamed, "Hard cheese!" Between them they made a lot of noise and presently there was a bang on the door and it burst open.

There stood Miss Brandy Brown, her eyes flashing even more than the sequins on her dress.

"*Will* you stop making such a row? I'm trying to rest after my performance," she said very crossly indeed.

The instant she opened the door, Isabella flew out through it like a feathered bullet, so that all Miss Brandy Brown saw inside the room was Arabel, looking perfectly tidy, and Mortimer, looking decidedly *un*tidy.

"If that bird makes any more disturbance I shall tell Captain Mainbrace that he's got to be shut up in a crate in the hold!" she said. Then she went out, slamming the door, and flounced back to her own cabin. She was not best pleased when, ten minutes later, Mike the steward tapped on the door and came in.

"It's just to fetch the tie, Miss," he said.

"Tie? What tie?"

"Tie for the young lady's raven next door," said Mike, taking it from the fridge and tiptoeing out again.

After that, relations were a bit strained between Mortimer the raven and Miss Brandy Brown.

3

On the second day at sea, luckily, the weather was calm, if rather foggy. Arabel spent a good deal of time in the games room, playing table tennis with Henry Mainbrace, the captain's son. This was fine, so long as they managed to keep a rally going and the ball stayed on the table. But Mortimer and Isabella were watching, perched like umpires on a convenient pile of folding deck chairs. Every time a ball went onto the floor either Isabella or Mortimer would swoop down and swallow it. By eleven o'clock each bird had swallowed so many balls that Henry declared he could hear them rattling inside.

"All those balls can't be good for them," Arabel said rather anxiously.

"No worse than having eggs inside you," Henry pointed out. "And lots of birds have those. Isabella laid an egg last month."

"Mortimer has never laid an egg," Arabel said.

Anyway, at this point Mr. Spicer, the steward who was in charge of the games room, came in, and when he discovered that Mortimer and Isabella between them had swallowed seventeen Ping-Pong balls, he said that was quite enough, and they had better go and play somewhere else or there would be none left for the other passengers.

They went and played with the fruit machines for a while, as Mortimer loved putting coins into slots. But nobody won anything, and presently they ran out of cash. Also, Mortimer was discovered posting a whole lot of potato crisps into a letter box labeled SUGGESTIONS.

"It's supposed to be for people who have good ideas for entertainment," said Henry.

"Now your father will think people want more potato crisps," said Arabel.

"Or not so many," said Henry. "Let's go out onto the promenade deck. We can get out through these sliding doors."

"Oughtn't we to put on our raincoats?" said

Arabel, who wasn't sure that Mortimer wanted to go outside.

Isabella definitely didn't want to go; she flew off in the direction of Lady Dunnage's cabin.

"It's only fog," said Henry. "Fog doesn't wet you."

Out on the big triangular deck to the rear of the games room everything looked very misty and mysterious. When Arabel and Henry walked right to the back, they could see the ship's wake, creaming away into the fog like two rows of white knitting. Arabel held tight on to Mortimer's leg in case he should be tempted to try flying. The ship was going so fast that if he did she was afraid he might be left behind. But Mortimer displayed no wish to fly; on the contrary, he did not seem at all interested in the sea. He huddled against Arabel's ear and muttered, "Hek-hek-hek," which was his way of informing her that he wanted to put on his tie.

As it happened, Arabel had the tie in her cardigan pocket. She pulled it out and waved it up and down in the cold, damp, foggy air until it was cool enough to satisfy Mortimer. Then she carefully wrapped it round and round him and walked along the deck carrying him wrapped up like a caterpillar in a cocoon with his eyes shut.

"I'm afraid he's not enjoying the trip very much," she said.

"He'll like it better when the weather gets hotter," Henry said.

They had come to a big flat square in the middle of the deck with a handle on it.

"What's that?" said Arabel. "It looks like the cover of a cheese dish."

"It is a cover," Henry said. "The swimming pool's under there. When the weather gets hot, they lift off that cover with a hoist and we can swim. The water's heated."

"I hope it gets warmer soon," said Arabel. "It isn't very hot now."

A few people were sitting out in deck chairs, but they were all wrapped up in thick rugs, like Mortimer in his tie.

Mr. Spicer came out with a trayful of steaming

cups and handed them round to the people in the chairs.

"What's that?" Arabel asked.

"Hot beef tea and cream crackers," said Henry.

Mortimer sniffed, opened one eye, and poked Arabel's ear to inform her that he wanted to try a cup of hot beef tea; however, when he had tasted a beakful of the stuff he decided that he did not like it and spat it out, making a very vulgar noise which caused all the ladies and gentlemen in the deck chairs to raise their eyebrows. He poked the cream cracker in among the folds of his tie.

Arabel and Henry walked on quickly, up some stairs, and along a narrower part of the deck toward the front end of the ship. Mortimer huddled down inside his tie and shut his eyes again.

"What are all those small boats hanging up there in a row?" Arabel asked.

"They're the lifeboats," Henry told her. "If the ship was wrecked, or someone fell overboard, they'd unhook the boats and slide them down those sloping things, which are called davits, into the sea."

"There don't seem to be very many boats; are there enough for all the passengers?" Arabel said.

"Each one holds thirty people and there are fifteen on each side."

"But how many people are there on the ship?"

That Henry didn't know.

Near the front end of the deck they came to another flight of steps leading up to a locked door.

"What's in there?" asked Arabel.

"That's the bridge, where they have all the controls and steer the ship," said Henry. "It's like the engine room of a train."

Arabel had never been in the engine room of a train, so that did not help.

"Well, it's like the dashboard of a car," said Henry. "I daresay my dad will let you go in and look at it sometime."

Just then a dreadful thing happened.

The nearer they got to the forward end of the ship, the harder the wind blew, because the ship was traveling fast and there was nothing to screen them; it was like standing up in an open car that is rushing along at sixty miles an hour.

When they reached the steps leading up to the

bridge, Mortimer opened an eye and looked about him. The first thing he noticed was a letter box slot in the locked door that said CAPTAIN. Before Arabel could stop him, he left her shoulder, scrabbled his way very fast, beak over claw, up the rail of the staircase, and posted his cream cracker, which had been tucked in among the folds of his tie, through the letter box.

Then he began to come down again. But the tie, probably loosened by the removal of the cream cracker, was suddenly dragged off his neck by the fresh wind. Quick as thought, before he could even let out a squawk, or Arabel could grab it, the wind whisked it away, over the deck rail and out of view.

"Oh, my goodness—," cried Arabel in utter dismay.

She and Henry rushed to the rail and looked over; but there was nothing to be seen. The fog was now so thick that they could see only a few yards down the side of the ship.

No tie.

It had taken a moment or two for Mortimer, clinging to the balustrade, to understand what had happened. He felt a draft, an unaccustomed chill round his middle. Then he realized that the reason why he felt so unwrapped was because his tie had disappeared. He let out a long and lamentable squawk.

"Kaaaaaark!"

"Oh, Mortimer, I'm *sorry*!" cried Arabel.

Mortimer gave her a look of frightful reproach. It said, plain as words, "What's the use of your sorrow to me? *That* won't keep me warm. Why didn't you tie the tie in a knot?"

Arabel picked up Mortimer and held him tight.

"I'd better take him back to our cabin," she said.

Henry kindly promised that he would ask his father to tell all the crew to keep a lookout for Mortimer's tie, just in case it had blown to another part of the ship and got tangled up in some bits of machinery.

"But I'm afraid it's most likely gone straight into the sea," he said.

Mortimer glared at him balefully.

Arabel carried Mortimer back to their room, stopping at the ship's shop on the way for a bag of raspberry jelly delights. Usually Mortimer was very fond of these, but at this moment he couldn't have cared less about them. Nor did he want to throw cards into the air and stab them with his beak, or any of the other activities that Arabel suggested. He made it plain that he wanted nothing but his tie. He croaked and flapped and moped and sulked and sat hunched in the upper bunk, looking miserably down at Arabel or out through the porthole at the heaving gray sea.

To make matters worse, the weather was becoming quite rough. The *Queen of Bethnal Green* was entering the Bay of Biscay, where the water comes rushing in from the Atlantic and bumps against the shore and bounces back and tosses passing ships up and down in a very disagreeable way.

The *Queen of Bethnal Green* began to tip up and down and to roll from side to side. Arabel found, presently, that all the lurching about made her feel rather queer; and as for Mortimer, he started to look decidedly unlike himself; if a bird of his complexion could be said to look green, then Mortimer looked it.

Arabel began to feel really anxious about him.

At last she pushed the red button to summon Mike the steward.

Mike, when he came, was cheerful and reassuring. He examined Mortimer, who was now sitting on Arabel's pink-blanketed bunk with his eyes closed.

"Feeling a bit all-overish, is he? You, too? Lots o' the passengers are, just now. It'll be better tomorrow when we get across the Bay. You'd better take a couple of Kwenches—they'll put you right in no time. Here you are—I always carry a few."

He brought out of his pocket a couple of large pale-green pills.

"There you are! Guaranteed to relieve any discomfort or travel sickness or indisposition due to climatic conditions."

"Oh, thank you, Mike. You are kind," said Arabel. She swallowed her pill with a glass of water.

"WARNING," said Mike, reading from the packet. "These tablets may cause drowsiness. If affected, be sure not to drive or operate machinery."

"Well, Mortimer and I aren't likely to be operating any machinery," said Arabel. "Unless you count the fruit machines. Mike, do you think this tablet is rather large for Mortimer? After all, he's only a bird. Should we cut it in half? Or even a quarter?"

"Maybe we better," said Mike. He dug into his white jangle pocket again and pulled out a collection of jingling things—keys, bottle openers, corkscrews, can openers, and a penknife. But before he could cut the pill in half with any of these tools, Mortimer, who had been peering at it through half-closed eyes for the last few minutes, suddenly opened his beak very wide indeed and swallowed it down. Then he shut his eyes again.

"Oh, well," said Mike. "I daresay he'll be all right. He's swallowed plenty odder things than that, if what I hear from Mr. Spicer is true. It'll probably just give him a good nap." He gathered up his keys and corkscrews.

Mortimer slightly opened his eyes and directed a hostile look at Mike's back, which was now turned to him, as the steward drew the curtains across the porthole to shut out the dismal view. Very neatly, and without making the slightest noise, Mortimer reached out a claw and hooked up a ring of keys which was dangling half out of Mike's pocket, and tucked it under his wing. Neither Mike nor Arabel observed this.

"I'd have a nap, too, if I was you," said Mike. "I'll bring you along some tea and sponge cakes by and by."

Arabel thought this was good advice. She curled up in her warm pink blankets and had a nap. Mortimer did, too, with the keys tucked safely under his wing.

When Arabel woke next, quite a lot of time had passed by. It was five o'clock. Mike had come back with the tea and sponge cakes. He had with him also a large selection of ties.

"Cap'n Mainbrace was sorry to hear from young Henry that your bird lost his comforter. He took up a collection among the ship's officers. This here's the result."

There were ties of every kind—spotted, striped, wool, satin, wide, narrow, plain, and bow. But no dark green tie.

"Oh, that's very kind of them," said Arabel. "Mortimer's still asleep. I'll show them to him as soon as he wakes up."

As a matter of fact, she was not too hopeful that Mortimer would like any of the ties, knowing how hard he was to please. But there would be no harm in trying.

"Let sleeping birds lie," said Mike. "I wouldn't rouse him till he wakes of hisself. I was to tell you that your ma's having her hair done in the beauty salon, and your pa's playing bingo."

Arabel certainly had no intention of rousing Mortimer.

She tiptoed away, leaving him still fast asleep, warmly cocooned in pink blankets. Just to be on the safe side, she locked the cabin door.

4

Arabel watched Mr. Jones playing bingo for a while, but she did not find it very interesting, and presently she went off with Henry, who came to tell her that a ship's treasure hunt was being organized and she had been invited to help lay the clues. They had just begun doing this on the fiesta deck when they heard loud screams coming from the direction of the beauty salon, which was not far away.

Screams always made Arabel anxious if Mortimer was anywhere in the neighborhood; so often they seemed to have some connection with him. She started off toward the beauty salon and saw Miss

Brandy Brown running down the stairs with half her hair in curlers and the other half loose and floating behind her.

"What is it?" Arabel asked. But Miss Brown rushed past without answering.

Then Mrs. Jones came out of the salon.

"Oh my stars, is that you, Arabel?" she said. "Why ever haven't you been keeping an eye on Mortimer? He came wandering into the beauty parlor as if he was under the affluence of incohol, gliding along with his eyes tight shut and his toes turned up and his wings stuck straight out before him, just like good Queen MacBess on her way to the Hampton Court Palais de Danse. It's my belief he's been magnetized by one of those hypopotanists."

"Oh dear," said Arabel. "I thought he was safe in my cabin fast asleep."

"He *was* fast asleep. That's what I mean!"

"Why was everybody screaming?"

"Well it wasn't everybody, dearie," said Mrs. Jones, "but only that Miss Brandy Brown, who, say what you like, is a very silly historical girl to fly off the handle just because she sees a bird walk past when she's sitting under the dryer; she says she's got an algebra about birds, or an agony—all he did was give her green towel a tweak—"

"Poor Mortimer," said Arabel, "I expect he was looking for his tie in his sleep."

"And then, of course, a bottle of setting lotion fell on him, and with the dryer on the floor, blowing, all his feathers turned curly, so he did look rather peculiar—"

"I'd better find him," said Arabel, and hurried off.

When she got to the beauty salon, Mortimer was not to be seen, though there was a fair amount of chaos which suggested that he had spent several minutes in there hunting for his tie; some dryers were knocked over and blowing hot air in every direction, taps were running, bottles were broken, green nylon overalls and towels lay all over the place, and there were enough scattered hairpins to build a model of the Eiffel Tower.

Henry joined Arabel and they began methodically hunting through the ship. They were partly helped and partly hindered by the public-address system.

"Will any member of the crew or passengers seeing a large raven, who doesn't answer to the name Mortimer and is apparently walking in his sleep and searching for a green tie, please contact Miss Arabel Jones in Cabin 1K on the upper deck."

"How could he have got out of your cabin? I thought you locked it," panted Henry as they ran along the promenade deck, examining all the tarpaulin-covered lifeboats to see if any of them seemed to have been disturbed lately.

"I don't understand it," said Arabel. "But I've heard that when people are walking in their sleep they can fall off very high places without being hurt. Perhaps they can go through locked doors, too."

She didn't know, of course, that Mortimer had Mike's bunch of passkeys, which would open any door on the ship. Nobody knew this until the *Queen of Bethnal Green* suddenly began sailing in circles.

"Losh sakes! What's come wi' the ship?" exclaimed old Mr. Fairbairn, the chief engineer, who had gone off duty and was having a cup of tea in the Rumpus Lounge. He dashed back to the bridge, where the door was swinging open and the second engineer, Hamish McTavish, with a very red face, was declaring:

"I swearr to goodness all I did was turrrn my back for aboot thirrrty seconds tae charrt the day's courrse, and yon black rrruffian had the lock picked and was in like a whirrlwind—"

Mr. Fairbairn roared over the public-address system, "Wull Miss Arrabel Jones come withoot delay tae the brreedge, whurr her rraven Morrtimer is mekking a conseederable nuisance o' himself?"

Arabel and Henry rushed to the bridge, but by the time they arrived Mortimer, in his somnambulistic search for his tie, had evidently decided that it was not there, and had left by way of a ventilator. Just after he did so a series of red and green rockets began to shoot up from the *Queen of Bethnal Green.*

"Och, mairrrcy, he must ha' set off the deestress signals when he was sairrching through yon bank o' sweetches," exclaimed Hamish McTavish, and began hastily sending out radio messages to cancel the message of the distress signals before a whole posse of passing ships should begin to take them seriously and come steaming to the rescue.

Now a new message sounded over the loudspeaker.

"Will Miss Arabel Jones please come to the first-class kitchen where her raven, Mortimer, walking in his sleep, has destroyed seventy-four pounds of iceberg lettuce?"

But long before Arabel and Henry had got to the kitchen, Mortimer had moved on, leaving a trail of green beans, spinach, brussels sprouts, angelica, broken plates, and irate cooks' assistants.

"Will Miss Arabel Jones please come to the casino, where a large black bird is wandering around the pool table in a dazed manner with a sprig of broccoli dangling from his beak?"

But by the time they reached the casino, Mortimer had departed, leaving a scene of torn green baize and snapped cues behind him.

"Will Miss Arabel Jones please come to the

Swedish gymnasium—the Finnish sauna—the Spanish bar—the Chinese laundry—the bank—the crèche—the card room—the library—the hospital—"

Mortimer was never there.

To add to the confusion, Isabella the parrot, not wanting to be left out of any excitement, had managed to escape from Lady Dunnage's cabin and was flying gaily about the ship; several times she was grabbed by people who thought she was a raven and that they would be rewarded for capturing her, but Isabella had a very neat left-beak uppercut combined with a right-claw hook which ensured that no one ever held her for long. Her activities added most unfairly to Mortimer's general unpopularity.

At last Arabel, worn out, was obliged to go to bed without having found him.

"Poor Mortimer," she said sadly. "I do hope he's got somewhere comfortable to spend the night."

About an hour after she had gone to bed, Arabel was roused by screams from the cabin next door.

Miss Brandy Brown had been woken by a sound, and had switched on her bedside light just in time to see Mortimer walk slowly through into her kitchenette, open the fridge, and peer gloomily inside. She was so paralyzed with astonishment that she did nothing until he had turned and was halfway across the room again. Then she jumped out of bed yelling: "Help! Murder! Thieves! Jackdaws! Magpies!"

By the time she had reached the door, Mortimer, as usual, had vanished from view.

She banged on Arabel's door.

"Have you got that bird in there with you?"

"No," said Arabel, anxiously opening up. "I only wish I had."

"Well, he was here just now. And I warn you," said Miss Brandy Brown ominously, "if he pesters me anymore, I shall take whatever steps seem proper."

"I don't see how taking steps will help," Arabel said, looking at the steps up to Mortimer's bunk.

"Anyway, Mortimer's usually the one who takes them."

But Miss Brown had flounced back to her own room.

It was a night of terror on board the *Queen of Bethnal Green.* People burst screaming from their cabins, they rushed in a panic out of lifts and got jammed in staircases; rumors flew about the ship far, far faster than Mortimer could have, even if he had had the speed of a vampire jet: "There's a mad raven on board—a bloodsucking vulture—a giant bat—it attacks any green article—beware!"

———

By next morning, luckily, the ship had got through the Bay of Biscay, the weather had turned sunny and hot, and the coast of Spain came into view.

Mortimer was nowhere to be seen, so everybody could relax except Arabel, who was more and more worried, terribly afraid that he might have fallen overboard, though she hoped, of course, that he had simply found some green thing that would do instead of his tie, and had curled up with it in a quiet corner for a good long nap.

Another person who wasn't happy was Mike the steward. Miss Brandy Brown had sent for him and given him a terrible telling off; she accused him of letting the raven into her cabin when he went in to turn down the bed. "For how else could he have got the door open?" she said. "He must have been lurking in my cabin for hours."

It was no use Mike's protesting he had done no such thing. She wouldn't listen, and he felt very ill used.

After lunch the *Queen of Bethnal Green* anchored off the coast of Spain. Boats came out from the land; anybody who liked could go ashore in them. Lots of passengers went, including Miss Brandy Brown and Mr. and Mrs. Jones. But Arabel said she would prefer to stay on board.

"Don't you want to see Spain, dearie?" said Mrs. Jones, who in secret thought it sadly probable that Mortimer had been lost overboard.

"No," said Arabel. "I shall go on hunting. And they're going to take the cover off the swimming pool and Henry's father is going to teach Henry and me to swim."

With light hearts, feeling that their child could hardly be in better hands, Mr. and Mrs. Jones went off to look at Spain.

Henry and Arabel watched the cover taken off the pool. At one side of the deck there was a small crane which was used for hoisting heavy objects on board, and now, with one of the crew winding its handle, the crane leaned forward and tweaked the big lid off the pool.

Arabel had a secret hope that perhaps Mortimer would be underneath, but he wasn't.

However, they had a very enjoyable swim with Henry's father. But presently the water in the pool began to tip and slop about a good deal, and the sky turned gray, and Captain Mainbrace, glancing up at it, said: "Looks like dirty weather coming. It's a good thing that the shore boats are due back."

He hurried off to check his instruments and listen to the weather forecast.

Henry and Arabel got dressed and then watched the entertainment staff, who were making ready for an open-air concert to be held on deck that evening.

The crane dropped the lid back over the swimming pool, and then the Rumpus Lounge piano was rolled as far as the doorway leading to the open deck. There, a rope was tied round it, and then the crane hooked its hook into the rope and picked up the piano as easily as if it had been a basket of potatoes (although it was a concert grand almost as large as Mr. Jones's taxi) and gently dropped it down right on top of the swimming pool lid.

While this was happening, some members of the entertainment staff were setting out potted palms and orange trees and blooming roses in tubs, and others were painting a huge piece of hardboard with a beautiful sunset scene. This was to go behind the piano so that it would look as if Miss Brown and the Stepney

Stepalives were performing in the middle of a Persian garden.

Arabel and Henry watched for a while and then they went off to hunt for Mortimer in all the places they hadn't tried yet. It was a great pity that they went away when they did, for not five minutes after they had gone below Mortimer himself came wandering out through the door from the games room, where he had been dozing behind a pile of deck chairs.

Just at that moment nobody was around. The scene painters had gone off to have their tea, and so had the piano shifters.

Mortimer meandered slowly along. A pot of lavender-colored paint had been knocked over, and he walked through a puddle of the stuff, leaving a trail of lavender footprints behind him. He was still fast asleep due to the powerful action of the green pill Mike had given him. He walked with his wings stretched out in front of him, as if he were feeling his way. When he came to the piano stool he climbed on it, and so on to the piano, and then, as if he had expected all along that it would be there waiting for him, got inside the open lid.

Then he lay down on the strings and went on sleeping.

It was just at this moment that Mike the steward came up on deck; he had finished his tea and wanted a breath of fresh air. The first thing he noticed was

the trail of lavender footprints leading to the piano.
Mike tiptoed up to the piano and looked inside.
There was Mortimer, lying on his back on the strings,
fast asleep, breathing peacefully, with his feet covered in lavender paint.

Quick as a flash, but very quietly, Mike shut the
piano lid and locked it.

His first intention had been to find Arabel and
tell her that her companion was safe. In fact, he did
start off to look for her. But he did not find her at
once (she was in the sauna room, right down at the

bottom of the ship). In the meantime, as he hunted for Arabel, Mike couldn't help thinking to himself: "Wouldn't it be a lark to leave Mortimer inside the piano till Miss Brandy Brown starts to play in the concert this evening! I bet he'd kick up a rumpus! Maybe that would teach snooty Miss B not to make such a fuss over things people didn't even do."

Mike was still feeling very ruffled and sore at the things Miss Brown had said to him.

5

The shore boats were coming back, and only just in time, for the sky was covered with fat black clouds and the wind was getting up, and so were the waves, and there was also a low rumble of thunder every now and then. And big drops of rain had begun to fall.

Captain Mainbrace sent a message to Miss Brandy Brown that her outdoor concert had better be altered to an indoor one, since he was going to hoist up anchor and take the *Queen of Bethnal Green* out to sea until the storm had blown over, to avoid the danger of being washed against the rocky coast.

So Miss Brown, in her turn, sent a message to the scene shifters, asking them if they would move the things back into the Rumpus Lounge; and, wiping the tea from their mouths and stubbing out their cigarettes, they came back on deck. Once more the crane was swung out, the hook was lowered, and the rope was knotted around the grand piano. The hook was tucked into the rope, and the piano was hoisted up into the air.

But just at that moment several things happened simultaneously. The siren let out a blast—*woooooooooooop*—the *Queen of Bethnal Green* started turning round, moving toward the open sea—and a huge wave, piled up by a giant gust of wind, which had been rolling along toward the liner, met her head-on and caused her to bounce from end to end like a floating sponge when somebody jumps into the bath.

What happened? The grand piano, at the end of its rope, swung violently sideways, like a conker on a string—there it was, a piano in midair, everybody staring at it; next minute the rope broke, *kertwang!* and there was the piano flying off as if it had been catapulted.

Mike the steward happened to look out through the Rumpus Lounge window and see the piano land in the water—otherwise this story might have ended differently.

"Ohmygawd! What's that piano doing out there in the sea?" he gasped, and rushed out on deck, where,

in the pouring rain, the crane operator was apologizing to Miss Brandy Brown and she was saying that playing on that piano was the next thing to playing on an old sardine can and she, for one, didn't care if it floated off to the Canary Islands; anyway, there must be another piano somewhere about the ship.

"B-b-b-b-b-b-but Miss B-b-b-b-b-b-b-brown! Mortimer the raven's inside that piano!" wailed Mike.

Arabel and Henry, who had heard the siren and felt the ship's violent lurch, and had come dashing up on deck to find out what was happening, arrived just in time to hear Mike say this and Miss Brandy Brown reply:

"Well, if that's so, I hope the perishing piano floats right over to Pernambuco with the blessed bird inside it."

But luckily for Mortimer, Mr. Fairbairn, the chief engineer, also happened to be passing just then. Henry grabbed his arm.

"Oh, Mr. Fairbairn! Arabel's raven is inside that piano!"

"Och, mairrcy, the puir bairrd—whit unchancy hirdumdirdum gar'd him loup intae sic an orra hauld at sic a gillravaging time? Yon corbie's randy cantrips aye fissell us a' frae yin carfuffle tae anither; forby he's no like tae win oot frae this splore the noo wi'oot sic a dose o' mirligoes as'll gar him gang mair kenspeckit frae noo on—bless us a', whit a clamjamfry!"

But while Mr. Fairbairn was grumbling and exclaiming in this manner, he was not wasting any time; he had raced along the deck and knocked out the pins that held one of the lifeboats, No. 16, in position; while he did so, Arabel, Mike, and Henry scrambled into it; Mr. Fairbairn jumped nimbly after them as the boat slid down from its davits and landed in the sea with a plunge and a bounce. Almost before they were in the water, Mike had started the boat's engine, which began to go *chug-chug-chug* in a reliable and comforting manner, and just as well, for, seen from down here, the waves looked as huge and black as a herd of elephants, while the sky was getting darker every minute, the thunder growled, the

wind shrieked, and lightning, from time to time, sil-
vered the tips of the wave crests.

"Where's the piano?" cried Arabel anxiously.
"Can you see it, Mr. Fairbairn? Is it still floating?"

It was not easy to keep the piano in view now that
they were down at its level. But back on the *Queen of
Bethnal Green* Hamish McTavish had told Captain
Mainbrace what was going on, and he helped them
by having rockets fired in the direction of the black
floating object—it now looked no larger than a
matchbox—which was all that could be seen of Mortimer and Miss Brandy Brown's Broadwood.

But lifeboat No. 16 chugged reliably on its way;
and at last they caught up with the piano. None too
soon; it was settling lower and lower in the water as
they overtook it.

"Suppose the water's got inside?" said Arabel.

"Ne'er fash yersel', lassie—I'm after hearing that
yon Broadwood craftsmen do a grand watertight job
o' cabinet-making."

The lifeboat was equipped with a hook for getting people out of the water, so while Mr. Fairbairn
steered, Henry hung over the side and managed to
hook the piano by the leg, while Arabel clung like
grim death on to Henry's feet, and Mike leaned over
until he was nearly cut in half by the edge of the boat
and, with frightful difficulty, unlocked the lid of the

piano—which, by great good fortune, was floating the right way up.

"Is Mortimer there?" Arabel asked faintly, who could see nothing as she was lying flat holding on to Henry's feet.

"He's there all right," said Mike, who had almost fractured his spine hoisting up Mortimer's very considerable weight from the sinking piano into the safety of the boat.

"Is—is—is he alive?"

"I reckon he's unconscious," Mike said. "We'd better give him a slug of brandy."

Mortimer lay flat on the bottom boards with his eyes shut and his lavender-colored feet sticking

straight out; from underneath his wing fell Mike's key ring.

"So he's the pilfering so-and-so that stole my keys," said Mike. "I might have guessed it. Getting me into all that trouble!"

But then he thought how easily Mortimer might have drowned, due to his own idea for a practical joke, and he knelt down by the motionless raven with the brandy flask from the lifeboat's first-aid box.

Just at that moment Mortimer, lying on his back, gave a loud, unmistakable snore. Even over the sound of the engine and the storm they heard it.

"Och, havers, will ye look at that," said Mr. Fairbairn. "The sackless sumph is still sleeping. For a' sakes, let's gang oor ways back to the ship afore he wakes up."

It took them much longer to get back to the ship, for all the time they had been rescuing Mortimer the *Queen of Bethnal Green* had been steaming full speed ahead for the open sea, since she did not dare stay close to the dangerous cliffs.

Mr. and Mrs. Jones had just got back on board when all this excitement began, and had been horrified to see the line of lavender-colored footprints leading along the deck to nowhere, and to learn that their only child was out in a tiny boat on that black and wicked sea on such a perilous quest. In fact, Mrs. Jones fainted dead away and had to be revived

with smelling salts and a hot-water bottle against the back of her neck.

By the time she had come to, lifeboat No. 16 had been hauled back on board, and Mrs. Jones clung to Arabel and hugged her and shook her and slapped her and laughed and cried and said that Arabel must promise never, *never* to go off again in a boat like that in the middle of such a storm.

"But I'd have to, Ma, if Mortimer was floating in the piano."

"I don't care! You shouldn't have gone, even if he was inside a harpsichord! Now go and have a hot bath this minute, and take that dratted bird with you!"

Luckily, all through this Mortimer went on sleep-ing. Arabel had a hot shower, and Mike brought her a delicious supper on a tray, and a whole lot of people came to congratulate her on the brave rescue, and on having Mortimer back safe and sound. All the previous events were forgiven and forgotten; Arabel, Mortimer, Henry, Mike, and Mr. Fairbairn were the most popular people on the ship.

And all this time Mortimer went on sleeping.

Then the best thing of all happened.

Mr. Fairbairn arrived, carrying a soggy, wet, nasty, messy, salty, sodden, draggled bit of dark green woolly material.

"Hoo are ye the noo, lassie?" he said. "No' the waur for yer boatie trip? When I was mekking a'

siccar wi' the lifeboat I fund yon clout, an' for a' it's sae droukit an' towzled I bricht it along tae speer is't yon birdie's neck rag, that a' the blether's bin aboot?"

"Oh, Mr. Fairbairn, it *is*! It's Mortimer's tie!" cried Arabel joyfully. "Oh, thank you, thank you! It must have blown up, not down, and got tangled in the davits! Oh, Mortimer *will* be pleased. It's lovely and wet and cold, too—just the way he likes it."

At this moment Mortimer opened one eye. The first thing he saw was his dirty, soggy, wet, draggled, salt-encrusted, sodden, beloved green necktie.

Mortimer gave a huge sigh of relief, which made his feathers all stick out sideways like the petals of a French marigold. (They looked rather like petals, too, for they were still all curly with setting lotion activated by the salt water.)

Arabel laid the end of the tie by Mortimer's beak, and he took hold of it with a sudden quick snap. Then, shutting his eyes again, he stood up and turned round and round half a dozen times until he was nicely wound up. Then he dug his head under his wing, lay down, and went back to sleep.

But Mr. Fairbairn gave a party, and Arabel and Henry and Isabella went to it and stayed up till all hours.

The last seven days of the cruise passed quickly. The weather was fine. Miss Brandy Brown gave her concert with the Stepney Stepalives. Arabel and Henry played a lot more table tennis. The *Queen of Bethnal Green* steamed back across the Bay of Biscay, up the English Channel, round the corner of Kent, and along the Thames. All this time Mortimer stayed asleep. Just occasionally he would open one eye. If it could see water going past outside the porthole, he shut it again.

Then, at last, when he opened his eye, he saw the streets of Tilbury going past through Mr. Jones's taxi window.

"Kaaaark!" said Mortimer. He opened both eyes. The streets were still there—beautiful, gray, rainy streets with houses and shops and traffic lights—no sea anywhere. Mortimer sat bolt upright on Arabel's lap. His black eyes began to sparkle.

"He's *so* glad to be home again," said Arabel.

"Didn't I say that going on a cruise to Spain would be a horrible mistake? Didn't I?" said Mr. Jones. He was driving his own taxi, which Mr. Murphy had kindly brought to the dock for him.

Just as they rolled to a stop in front of Number Six, Rainwater Crescent, Mortimer clambered onto the back of the front seat. He reached over Mr. Jones's shoulder and pulled the key out of the ignition. Then he flopped out through the taxi door (which Arabel had just opened) and made his way quite fast along the pavement.

"Stop him, *stop him!*" said Mr. Jones. "That bunch has the front-door key on it, too."

But before Arabel could get to him, Mortimer had reached up, tip-claw, and posted the whole bunch of keys into the open slot of the letter box that stood in front of Number Six.

Then he happily climbed up the front steps, dragging his tie behind him.

The Spiral Stair

1

"Excuse me. Are you two gentlemen going as far as Foxwell?" Mrs. Jones inquired nervously, having opened the railway carriage door and poked her head through. The hand that was not holding the door handle clasped the wrist of Mrs. Jones's daughter, Arabel, who was carrying a large canvas bag.

Mrs. Jones had been opening doors and asking this question all the way along the train when she thought the occupants of the carriage looked respectable. Some of them did not. Some weren't going as far as Foxwell.

But the two men in this carriage looked *very* respectable. Both had bowler hats. One was small and stout, one was large and pale. Their briefcases were in the rack, and they were talking to each other in low, confidential, businesslike voices.

Now they stopped and looked at Mrs. Jones as if they were rather put out at being interrupted. But one of them—the small fat one—said, "Yes, madam. We are getting out *at* Foxwell, as it happens."

The other man, the large pale one, frowned, as if he wished his friend had not been so helpful.

"Oh, are you, that's ever such a relief then," cried Mrs. Jones, "for you look like nice reliable gentlemen and I'm sure you won't mind seeing that my little girl, that's Arabel here, gets out at Foxwell where her uncle Urk will be meeting her and I know it looks ever so peculiar my not going with her myself, but I have to hurry back to Rumbury Hospital where my hubby, Mr. Jones, is having his various veins seen to and he likes me to visit him all the visiting hours and I couldn't leave poor little Arabel alone at home every day, let alone Mortimer, and my sister Brenda isn't a *bit* keen to have them, but luckily my hubby's brother Urk lives in the country and said he would oblige, leastways it was his wife, Effie, that wrote but Ben said Urk would know how to manage Mortimer on account of him being used to all kinds of wild—"

Luckily, at this moment the guard blew a shrill blast on his whistle, for the two men were beginning to look even more impatient, so Mrs. Jones hastily bundled Arabel into the railway carriage and dumped her suitcase on the seat beside her.

"Now you'll be ever such a good girl, won't you dearie, and Mortimer, too, if he *can,* and take care among all those megadilloes and jumbos and do what

Aunt Effie says—and we'll be down to fetch you on Friday fortnight—"

Here the guard interrupted Mrs. Jones again by slamming the carriage door, so Mrs. Jones blew kisses through the window as the train pulled away. One of the bowler-hatted men—the short fat one— got up and put Arabel's case in the rack, where she couldn't reach it to get out her picture book. He would have done the same with the canvas bag she was carrying, but she clutched that tightly on her lap, so he sat down again.

The two men then took their hats off, laid them on the seat, settled themselves comfortably, and went on with their conversation, taking no notice whatever of Arabel, who was very small and fair-haired, and who sat very quietly in her corner.

After a minute or two she opened the canvas bag, out of which clambered a very large untidy black bird—almost as big as Arabel herself—who first put himself to rights with his beak, then stood tip-claw on Arabel's lap and stared out of the window at the suburbs of London rushing past.

He had never been in a train before and was so astonished at what he saw that he exclaimed, *"Nevermore!"* in a loud, hoarse, rasping voice which had the effect of spinning round the heads of the two men as if they had been jerked by wires. They both stared very hard at Arabel and her pet.

"What kind of a bird is that?" asked one of them, the large pale one.

"He's a raven," said Arabel, "and his name's Mortimer."

"Oh!" said the pale man, losing interest. "Quite a *common* bird."

"Mortimer's not a bit common," said Arabel, offended.

"Well, I hope he behaves himself on this train," said the pale man, and then the two men went back to their conversation.

Mortimer, meanwhile, looked up and saw Arabel's suitcase in the rack above his head. As soon as he saw it he wanted to get up there, too. But Arabel could not reach the rack, and Mortimer was not prepared to fly up. He disliked flying and very rarely did so if he could find somebody to lift him. He now said, "Kaark" in a loud, frustrated tone.

"Excuse me," said Arabel very politely to the two men, "could you please put my raven up in the rack?"

This time both men looked decidedly irritated at being interrupted.

"Certainly not," said the large pale one.

"Rack ain't the place for birds," said the short fat one. "No knowing *what* he might not get up to there."

"By rights he ought to be in the guard's van," said the first. "Any more bother from you and we'll call the guard to take him away."

They both stared hard and angrily at Arabel and Mortimer, and then began talking to each other again.

"We'd better hire a truck in Ditchingham—Fred will be there with the supplies; he can do it—have the truck waiting at Bradpole crossroads—you carry the tranquilizers, I'll have the nets—twenty ampoules ought to be enough, and a hundred yards of netting—"

"Don't forget the foam rubber—"

"Nevermore," grumbled Mortimer to himself, very annoyed at not getting what he wanted the instant he wanted it.

"Look at the sheep and the dear little lambs in that field, Mortimer," said Arabel, for the train had now left London and was running through green country. But Mortimer was not the least interested in dear little lambs. While Arabel was watching them, he very quietly and neatly hacked one of the men's bowler hats into three pieces with his huge beak and then swallowed the bits in three gulps. Neither of the men noticed what he had done. They were deep in plans.

"*You* take care of the ostriches—mind, they kick—and *I'll* look after the zebras."

"They kick, too."

"Just have to be quick with the tranquilizer, that's all."

Mortimer, coming to the conclusion that nobody was going to help him, hoisted himself up into the rack with one strong shove-off and two flaps. The men were so absorbed in their plans that they did not notice this either.

"Here's a map of the area—the truck had better park here, by the ostrich enclosure—"

Mortimer, up above them, suddenly did his celebrated imitation of the sound of a milk truck rattling along a cobbled street. *"Clinketty-clang, clang, clink, clanketty clank."*

Both men glanced about them in a puzzled manner.

"Funny," said the short fat man, "could have sworn I heard a milk truck."

"Don't be daft," said the large pale one. "How could you hear a *milk cart* in a *train*? Now—we have to think how to get rid of the watchman—"

Mortimer now silently worked his way along the rack until he was over the men's heads. He wanted to have a look at their luggage. From one of the two flat black cases there stuck out a small thread of white down. Mortimer took a quiet pull at this. Out came a straggly piece of ostrich feather. Mortimer studied the bit of plume for a long time, sniffed at it, listened to it, and finally poked it under his wing. Presently, forgetting about it, he hung upside down from the rack, swaying to and fro with the motion of the train, and breathing deeply with pleasure.

"Please take care, Mortimer," said Arabel softly.

Mortimer gave her a very carefree look. Then, showing off, he let go with one claw. However, at that moment the train went over a set of switches— *kerblunk*—and Mortimer's hold became detached. He fell, heavily.

By great good luck, Arabel, who was anxiously watching, saw Mortimer let go, and so she was able, holding wide the two handles of the canvas bag, to catch him—he went into the bag headfirst.

The ostrich plume drifted to the floor.

The two men, busy with their plans, noticed nothing of this.

The fat one was saying, "The giraffes are the most important. Reckon we should pack them in first? They take up most room."

"Nah, can't. Giraffes have to be *un*loaded first. They're wanted by a costumer in Woking."

"Why the blazes should somebody want *giraffes* in *Woking*?"

"How should *I* know? Not our business, anyway."

Mortimer poked his head out of the canvas bag. He was very annoyed at his mortifying fall, and ready to make trouble if possible. His eyes lit on the second bowler hat.

Fortunately, at this moment the train began to slow down.

"Nearly at Foxwell now, little girl," said the fat man. He took down Arabel's case and put it by her on the seat.

"You being met here?" he said.

"Yes," said Arabel. "My uncle Urk is meeting me. He is—" But the two men weren't paying any attention to her. The large one was looking for his hat.

"Funny, I put it just here. Where the devil could it have got to?"

"Oh dear," said Arabel politely, when no hat could be found. "I'm afraid my raven may have eaten it. He *does* eat things sometimes."

"Rubbish," said the hatless man.

"Don't be silly," said the fat man.

Now the train came to a stop, and Arabel, through the window, saw her uncle Urk on the platform. She waved to him and he came and opened the door.

"There you are, then," he said. "Enjoy your trip? This all your luggage?"

Uncle Urk was brown and wrinkled, with a lot of bristly gray hair. There were bits of straw clinging to his clothes.

"Yes, thank you, Uncle Urk."

"That's right." He took Arabel's case, and she carried the bag with Mortimer in it. "Good-bye," she called to the two men, but they were still busy hunting for the lost hat.

"Look at this!" the pale one said angrily to the thin one, finding the bit of ostrich plume on the floor. "You careless fool!" He quickly picked up the feather and stuck it in his pocket.

Uncle Urk dropped Arabel's case in the back of his pickup truck and settled her and Mortimer in the front seat.

"Well? You excited at the thought of staying in a zoo?" he inquired.

"Yes, thank you," said Arabel. "Mortimer is, too, aren't you, Mortimer?"

"Kaaark," said Mortimer.

2

"D o you keep *every* kind of animal in your zoo, Uncle Urk?" Arabel asked.

"It ain't my zoo really, Arabel, you know. I'm just the head warden, and your aunt Effie runs the cafeteria," said Uncle Urk. "The zoo belongs to Lord Donisthorpe."

"Does he have lions and tigers?"

"No, he hasn't got any of those. He likes grass-eating animals mostly—wildebeests and zebras and giraffes. And birds and snakes. And he's got porcupines and a hippopotamus and a baby elephant. I expect you'll enjoy giving the baby elephant doughnuts."

"I thought they liked buns best?" said Arabel.

"Lord Donisthorpe has invented a doughnut-making machine," said her uncle. "It uses whole wheat flour and sunflower oil and honey, so the doughnuts it makes are very good for the animals. And so they blooming well oughter be at thirty pence apiece," he muttered to himself. "Cor! Did you ever? Six bob for a perishing doughnut!"

His truck at that moment passed between the gates in a high wire-mesh fence. Arabel noticed a sign that said CAUTION, ZEBRA CROSSING.

Ahead of them lay a ruined-looking castle, inside a moat, and a lot of wooden and stone buildings and haystacks. But Uncle Urk pulled up in front of a small white house with a neat garden around it. "Here's your aunt Effie and Chris Cross," he said.

Chris was a boy who used to live next door to Arabel's family in Rumbury Town, London. But he had come down to work in Lord Donisthorpe's zoo as a holiday job last summer, and liked it so much that he stayed on.

Aunt Effie was thin-faced and fuzzy-haired; her eyes were pale blue but sharp. Nearly all her remarks about people began with the words "You can't blame them—" which really meant that she *did* blame them, very much. "You can't blame the kids who drop their ice-cream wrappers; they've never learned no better, nasty little things. You can't blame murderers, it's their nature; what I say is, they ought to make them into pet food. You can't blame your uncle Urk for being such a muddler; he was born that way."

Now Aunt Effie's pale blue eyes snapped as she looked at Mortimer clambering out of his canvas bag, and she said, "Well, I s'pose you can't blame Martha for sending that monster down with Arabel. *I* wouldn't leave him alone in the house myself, wouldn't keep him a day, but so long as he stays in *my* house he stops inside the meat safe, that's the place for him!"

She fetched a galvanized zinc cupboard with a perforated door into the front hall and said to Arabel, "Put the bird in there!"

"Oh, *please* not, Aunt Effie," said Arabel, horrified. "Mortimer would hate that, he really would! He's used to being out. I'll keep an eye on him, I promise."

"Well, the very first thing he pokes or breaks with that great beak of his," said Aunt Effie, "into the meat safe he goes!"

Mortimer looked very subdued. He sat beside Arabel at tea, keeping quite quiet, but Arabel managed to cheer him up by slipping pieces of Aunt Effie's lardy-cake to him. It was very delicious — chewy and crunchy, with pieces of buttery toffeelike sugar in among the dough, and a lot of currants.

After tea, Aunt Effie had to go back to manage the cafeteria. Chris said, "I'm going to feed the giraffes, so I'll show Arabel over the zoo a bit, shall I?"

"Mind she's not a nuisance," said Aunt Effie.

Uncle Urk, who was also going to feed animals, said he would probably meet them near the camel house.

Lord Donisthorpe's zoo was in the large park which lay all round his castle. Lord Donisthorpe lived in the castle, which was in bad repair. The animals mostly lived in the open air, roaming about eating the grass. They had wooden huts and stone houses for cold weather or to sleep in. Builders were putting up more of these. They were also at work building an enormously high stone wall to replace the wire-mesh fence round the park.

"Is that to stop the animals escaping?" asked Arabel.

"No, they don't want to escape. They like it here," said Chris. "It's to stop thieves getting in. There have been a lot of robberies from zoos lately. When this one was smaller, Lord Donisthorpe just used to leave Noah the boa loose at night, and he took care of any thieves that got in. But now the zoo's getting so big there's too much ground to cover— Noah can't be everywhere at once."

Just at that moment Mortimer's eye was attracted by a beautiful stretch of wet cement which the builders had just laid. It was going to be the floor of the new porcupine palace. Quick as lightning Mortimer flopped off Arabel's shoulder and walked across the cement, leaving a trail of deeply indented bird prints.

"Gerroff there, you black buzzard!" shouted a workman, and he threw a trowel at Mortimer, who, startled, flew up into the nearest dark hole he could find. This happened to be the mouth of the cement mixer, which was turning round and round.

"Oh, please, quick, stop the mixer!" cried Arabel. "Please get him out!"

A confused sight of feet and tail feathers could be seen sticking out of the mixer. The man who was running it stopped the engine that turned the hopper and tipped it so that it pointed downward. Out came a great slop of half-mixed cement, and Mortimer, so coated over that nothing could be seen of him but his feet and black feathery trousers.

"We'd best pour a bucket of water over him before it sets," said Chris, and did so. "Lucky your aunt Effie wasn't around when *that* happened," he added, as Mortimer, croaking and gasping, reappeared from under the cement. "That'd be *quite* enough to get him shut up in the meat safe."

"Mortimer, you *must* be *careful* here," said Arabel anxiously.

Mortimer might have been put out by his mishap with the cement mixer—things like that often made him very bad-tempered—but luckily his attention was distracted just then by the sight of a herd of zebras, all black and white stripes.

"Nevermore!" he said, utterly amazed, staring with all his might as the zebras strolled across the road.

Then they passed a group of ostriches, who looked very vague and absentminded, as ostriches do, and were preening themselves in a patch of sand. When he was close by them, Mortimer did his celebrated imitation of an ambulance rushing past with bell clanging and siren wailing.

All the ostriches immediately stuck their heads in the sand.

"You better tell Mortimer not to make that noise in your aunt Effie's house," said Chris. "Your aunt Effie doesn't like noise."

Now they passed a cage which had an enormous sleepy-looking, greedy-looking snake inside it. "That's Noah the boa," said Chris. "He's very fond of doughnuts. Want to give him one?"

Arabel did not much care for the look of Noah the boa, but she did want to see how the doughnut machine worked. There was one near Noah's cage. It had a glass panel in front and a slot for putting in a tenpenny piece.

"The public has to put in three coins to get a doughnut," said Chris, "but luckily there's a lever behind that only zoo staff know about, so we can get ours for one. You have to put in one tenpenny piece to get it started; after that you keep pulling the lever."

He dropped a coin in the slot. Instantly an uncooked doughnut rolled down a chute into a pan of boiling oil behind the glass panel and began to fry. After a minute or two, a wire hook fished it out of the oil and held it up to dry.

"Now, if you were a member of the public, you'd have to put in another coin to get it sugared," said Chris. "But as we're zoo staff we can pull the lever." He did so, and a puffer blew a cloud of honey crystals all over the doughnut so that it became fuzzed with white.

"Now what happens?" said Arabel.

"Now, if you were a member of the public you'd have to put in a third coin to get it out," said Chris. He pulled the lever again. The hook let go of the doughnut, which rolled down another chute and was delivered into a crinkled paper cupcake case.

Mortimer, who had been watching all this with extreme interest, took a step forward along Arabel's arm. But Noah the boa had also been watching—at the first clank of the coin in the machine all his sleepiness had left him—and as Arabel took the doughnut from the paper cup, he opened his mouth so wide that his jaws were in a straight line up and down. Arabel rather timidly tossed in the doughnut, and Noah's jaws shut with a snap.

"His jaws are hinged so that he can swallow an animal as big as a pig if he wants to," said Chris. "But he prefers doughnuts; they are his favorite food."

"How do you know?" said Arabel. "He doesn't *look* pleased."

"Things he doesn't like he spits out," said Chris.

"Kaaark," said Mortimer in a gloomy, aggrieved tone.

"All right, Mortimer," said Arabel. "Ma gave me some money, so I'll do a doughnut for you now if Chris doesn't mind pulling the levers."

She dropped in her coin, and another raw doughnut slid into the boiling oil.

Mortimer's eyes shone at the sight, and he began to jump up and down on Arabel's shoulder.

When the doughnut was cooked and sugared, Chris pulled the lever to release it into the paper cup.

"Suppose a person only had two tenpenny pieces?" said Arabel.

"Then they better not start, or they'd have to go off and leave the doughnut waiting there for the next customer," said Chris. "But that doesn't often happen. Who'd be such a mug as to leave twenty pence's worth of doughnut for someone else to pick up for only ten?"

Just as Mortimer's doughnut came out, something unfortunate happened. A small head on a very long spotted neck came gently over Arabel's shoulder and nibbled up the doughnut so fast and neatly and quietly that for a moment Mortimer could not believe that it had gone. Then he let out a fearful wail of dismay.

"Nevermore!"

"Oh dear," said Chris. "That's Derek. These giraffes are just mad about doughnuts. If they see anybody near the machine, they come crowding round."

Arabel turned and, sure enough, three giraffes had come silently up behind them and were standing in a ring, evidently hoping that more doughnuts were going to be served.

"Their names are Wendy, Elsie, and Derek," Chris said.

"I'm *dreadfully* sorry, Mortimer," Arabel said. "I haven't any more money."

Neither had Chris.

Mortimer made not the least attempt to conceal his disappointment and indignation. He jumped up and down, and he screamed terrible words at the giraffes, who looked at him calmly and affably.

"What the dickens is the matter with that bird?" asked Uncle Urk, passing by with a bucket of wildebeest food.

"Derek ate his doughnut," said Chris.

"Well, for the land's sake, give him another," said Uncle Urk, who was very good-natured. "Here's ten pence."

"Oh, thank you, Uncle Urk," said Arabel. This time she pulled the levers, for Chris had to get on with his evening jobs.

When the doughnut came down the chute, Mortimer, who had been watching like a sprinter waiting for the tape to go down, lunged in and grabbed it just before Wendy could bend her long neck down.

He was so pleased with himself at having got in ahead of Wendy that, contrary to his usual habit, he rose up in the air, holding the doughnut in his beak, and flew vengefully and provokingly round and round the high heads of the giraffes.

"Mortimer, stop it! That isn't kind," said Arabel. "Just eat your doughnut and don't tease."

Mortimer took no notice. He swooped between Derek and Wendy, who banged their heads together as they both tried to snatch the doughnut. This amused Mortimer so much that by mistake he let go of the doughnut—which fell to the ground and was seized and swallowed by Elsie.

Mortimer drew a great breath of fury; all his feathers puffed out like a fancy chrysanthemum.

However, Arabel grabbed him and said, "That just serves you right, Mortimer. I haven't any more money, so you'll have to go without a doughnut now. Come along, we'd better go and see some more of Uncle Urk's zoo."

She walked on, but Mortimer was very displeased indeed, and kept looking back at the giraffes and muttering, "Nevermore, nevermore, nevermore" under his breath.

Then they met Lord Donisthorpe, the owner of the zoo. He was a tall, straggly man who looked not unlike his own giraffes and ostriches, except that he was not spotty and had no tail feathers. He had a very long neck, untidy white hair, and a vague expression.

"Ah, yes," he said, observing Arabel over the tops of his glasses, which were shaped like segments of orange. "You must be Mr. Jones's niece, come to stay. I hope you are enjoying your visit. But your raven seems out of spirits."

This was an understatement. Mortimer was now shrieking, "Nevermore!" at the top of his lungs, and spinning himself round and round on one leg.

"One of the giraffes ate his doughnut," Arabel explained.

"Perhaps he would like an ice cream in the cafeteria?" inquired Lord Donisthorpe. "Perhaps you would, too? They are very good. We make our own."

"Thank you, we should both like that very much," said Arabel politely.

On the way to the cafeteria they passed an immensely tall building made of wood and glass. "That is my new giraffe house," said Lord Donisthorpe.

At the word *giraffe* Mortimer looked ready to bash anyone who came near him.

The giraffe house was built to suit the shapes of the giraffes, with high windows, so that they could see out, and a spiral staircase in the middle, leading to a circular gallery, so that visitors could climb up and be on a level with the giraffes' faces. The walls of the building were not finished yet; one side was open. Mortimer looked very sharply at the spiral stair, and Arabel kept a firm hold of his leg, for he had been known to eat stairs on several occasions in the past. However, these stairs were made of ornamental ironwork, and it seemed likely that even Mortimer would find them tough.

"Come on, Mortimer, Lord Donisthorpe's going to buy you an ice cream," Arabel said.

"Kaaark," said Mortimer doubtfully.

The cafeteria, just beyond the giraffe house, had another doughnut machine by its door. Mortimer stared at this very hard as they walked by, but Lord Donisthorpe led the way into the cafeteria itself, which had red tables and shiny metal chairs and a counter with orange and lemon and coffee machines and piles of things to eat. Aunt Effie was at the counter, standing behind a glass case filled with cream cheese patties and toffee-covered carrots on sticks.

"We make our own toffee carrots," said Lord Donisthorpe. "They are very wholesome indeed. And we have three different flavors of homemade ice cream: dandelion, black currant, and quince. Which would you prefer?"

Arabel chose the quince, which was a beautiful orange-red color; Mortimer indicated that he would like the dandelion, which was bright yellow.

Aunt Effie gave them a disapproving look. "*I* don't know; eating again only half an hour after they had their tea," she muttered, scooping out the ice cream and ramming it into cones. "But I s'pose you can't blame them, brought up by that empty-headed Martha."

While she was serving out the ice cream, Mortimer noticed that an empty tray had been left at one end of the cafeteria rail.

Flopping off Arabel's shoulder onto the tray, he gave himself a powerful push-off with his tail and shot along the rail past the counter as if he had been on a toboggan, shouting, "Nevermore!" and spreading his wings out wide. His left-hand wing knocked a whole row of cream cheese patties into the black currant ice-cream bin.

Aunt Effie let out a shriek of rage. "How Martha can stand that fiend of a bird in her house I do not

TRY OUR DELICIOUS TOFFEE CARROTS

know!" she said. "Ben did warn Urk that he was a real menace, into every kind of mischief, and I can see he didn't exaggerate. Six patties and seventy-five pence's worth of black currant ice! You take him straight back to the house, Arabel Jones, and put him in the meat safe, and there he stays till Ben and Martha come to fetch you."

The various customers sitting at the little red plastic tables were greatly interested in all this excitement, and many heads turned to look at Mortimer, who had ended up jammed headfirst in the knife-and-fork rack at the end of the counter, and was now yelling loudly to be released.

Luckily it turned out that Lord Donisthorpe was very fond of cream cheese patties with black currant ice cream.

"Here," he said, handing Arabel the red and yellow ice-cream cones which he had been holding. "You take these while I find some more money. There you are, Mrs. Jones, this will pay for the damaged patties and all the ice cream with which they came in contact; pray put them all on a large plate, and then I will eat them, which will save my having to boil myself an egg later. Now—if I just remove the raven from the knife rack—I do not believe that any more need be said about this matter."

Aunt Effie looked as if she violently disagreed, but since Lord Donisthorpe was the owner of the zoo, she was obliged to give way. Mortimer was much too busy to trouble his head about the furious glances Aunt Effie was giving him; released from the knife rack, he sat on the red plastic table between Arabel and Lord Donisthorpe, holding his dandelion ice-cream cone in his claw and studying it admiringly. Then he ate it very fast in one bite and two swallows—crunch, hoosh, swallop—and then he looked round to see what everybody else was doing. Arabel had mostly finished her quince ice cream—which was delicious—but Lord Donisthorpe still had quite a number of cream cheese patties to go, so Mortimer helped him with four of them.

Meanwhile, at a table by the window, two men, one of them wearing a hat and one not, had been watching this scene, and were now staring thoughtfully at Mortimer.

The hatless man took his teacup and went back to the counter to have it refilled. "That seems to be a very badly behaved bird," he said to Aunt Effie as she handed him his cup and he gave her the money.

"You can say that again," snapped Aunt Effie. "He has to stay in my house while my brother-in-law has his veryclose veins operated on, but I certainly intend to see he does as little damage as possible while he's here. The havoc that monster has wreaked at my brother-in-law's you'd never believe—eaten whole gas stoves and kitchen sinks, he has—worse than a tribe of Tartar sorcerers, he is! Into the meat safe he goes the minute he gets back to my house, I can tell you."

"A very sensible plan, madam," the hatless man agreed. "And if I were you, I should put that meat safe out of doors. A bird like that can harbor all sorts of infection—it would be downright dangerous to have it in the house."

"That's true," said Aunt Effie. "We could all come down with Raven Delirium, or get Inter-citycosis from him. I'll put the meat safe out on the front lawn. And if it rains, so much the better; I don't suppose that black fiend ever had a wash in his life."

The hatless man went back to the window table with his tea. While he was waiting for it to cool, he said to his friend in a low voice, "We can pin the blame on the bird. All we have to do is to open the meat safe. Everybody will think that *he* let out the animals."

Presently the two men left the cafeteria and strolled away, glancing carelessly at the giraffe house, the zebra bower, and the ostrich haven as they passed. Then they left the zoo.

Arabel thanked Lord Donisthorpe for her and Mortimer's treats. Lord Donisthorpe patted her head and gave her a tenpenny piece. "That will buy your raven another doughnut," he said. "But I should wait till tomorrow."

"Oh yes, he's full up now," said Arabel.

Mortimer, absolutely stuffed with ice cream and cheese patty, made no difficulty about going home to bed.

"I'll be back at the house in twenty minutes," called Aunt Effie from the counter, where she was washing up the used knives and forks. "Don't you let that bird touch *anything* in the house. Tell your uncle Urk I said so."

Going toward home, Arabel and Mortimer caught

up with Uncle Urk, whose jobs were finished and who was intending to watch television.

"Uncle Urk," said Arabel, "I think those two men who were in the cafeteria are animal thieves. They were in the same railway carriage with me and Mortimer, and they were talking about zebras and giraffes and ostriches."

"*Course* they were talking about zebras and giraffes and ostriches, Arabel dearie," said Uncle Urk kindly. "'Cos they was a-coming to the zoo, see? Natural, people talks about zebras and camels and giraffes when they're a-going to *see* ostriches and giraffes and camels."

"I think they were thieves," said Arabel. "Don't you think so, Mortimer?"

"Kaaark," said Mortimer.

"Can't take what that bird says as evidence," said Uncle Urk. "'Sides, little gals gets to fancying things, *I* know. Little gals is very fanciful creatures. That's what you bin a-doing, Arabel dearie—you got to fancying things about animal thieves. We won't mention it to your aunt Effie, eh, case she gets nervous? Terrible nervous your aunt Effie can get, once she begins."

"But, Uncle Urk," said Arabel.

"Now, Arabel dearie, don't you trouble your head about such things—*or* mine," said Uncle Urk, who was dying to watch Rumbury Wanderers play Liverpool United, and he hurried into the house.

3

Arabel saw that Chris, whose evening jobs were finished, had taken his guitar into Uncle Urk's garden. Arabel and Mortimer loved listening to Chris play, so they went and sat beside him and he sang:

"Arabel's raven is quick on the draw,
Better steer clear of his beak and his claw,
When there is trouble, you know in your bones,
Right in the middle is Mortimer Jones!"

Mortimer drew himself up and looked immensely proud that a song had been written about him. Arabel sucked her finger and leaned against an apple tree.

Inside the house, Uncle Urk suddenly thought, "What if Arabel was right about those men being giraffe thieves? Ben says she's mostly a sensible little thing. I'd look silly if she'd a-warned me, and I didn't do anything, and they really *was* thieves."

So, after thinking about it for a while, he rang up Sam Heyward, the night watchman, on the zoo's internal telephone. "Sam," he said, "I got a kind of feeling there might be a bit o' trouble tonight, so why don't you let old Noah loose? It's months since he had a night out. You never know, if there's any miscreants about, he might put a spoke in their wheel."

"Okay, Urk, if you say so," said Sam. "Anyways, old Noah might catch a few rabbits; there's a sight too many rabbits about in the park just now, eating up all the wildebeest food."

Sam left his night watchman's hut to let out Noah the boa, who was very pleased to have the freedom of the park again, and slithered quietly away through the grass. When Sam returned to his hut, he didn't notice that a small tube had been slipped under the door, in the crack at the hinge end. As soon as he shut the door, a sweet-smelling gas began to dribble in through the tube. By slow degrees Sam became drowsier and drowsier until, after about half an hour, he toppled right off his stool and lay on the matting fast asleep, dreaming that he had put ten pounds on a horse in the Derby called Horseradish, and that it had been on the point of winning when Noah the boa, who could travel at a terrific speed when he chose to, suddenly shot under the tape just ahead of Horseradish and won the race.

Meanwhile, in Uncle Urk's garden Chris sang,

"Arabel's raven is perfectly hollow,
What he can't chew up he'll manage to
*   swallow—*
Furniture—fire escapes—fencing—and
*   phones—*
All are digested by Mortimer Jones."

Mortimer looked even prouder.
Chris sang,

"When the ice cream disappears from the cones,
When you are deafened by shrieks or by moans,
When the fur's flying, or the air's full of stones,
You can be certain—"

Just at this moment Aunt Effie came home. As soon as she was through the gate, she said, "Chris! Fetch out that meat safe!"

Looking rather startled, Chris laid down his guitar and did as he was told. He placed the meat safe under the apple tree.

Instantly, Aunt Effie grabbed Mortimer, thrust him into the safe (which he completely filled), shut the door, and slammed home the catch.

A fearful cry came from inside.

"There!" said Aunt Effie. "Now, you go up to bed, Arabel Jones, and I don't want to hear a *single sound* out of you, or out of that bird, till morning—do you hear me?"

Since Mortimer, inside the meat safe, was making a noise like a troop of roller skaters crossing a tin bridge and shouting, "Nevermore!" at the top of his lungs, it was quite hard for Arabel to hear what Aunt Effie said, but she could easily understand what her aunt meant.

Arabel went quietly and sadly up to bed, but she had not the least intention of leaving Mortimer to pass the night inside the meat safe. "He hasn't done anything bad in Aunt Effie's house," Arabel thought, "so why should he be punished by being shut inside the meat safe? It isn't fair. Besides, Mortimer can't *stand* being shut up."

Indeed, the noise from the meat safe could be heard for two hundred yards around Uncle Urk's house. But Aunt Effie went indoors and turned up the volume of the television very loud in order to drown Mortimer's yells and bangs.

"When he learns who's master he'll soon settle down," she said grimly.

Arabel always did exactly as she was told. Aunt Effie had said, "I don't want to hear a single sound out of you," so, as soon as it was dark, and Aunt Effie and Uncle Urk had gone to bed, Arabel put on her dressing gown and slippers and went very softly down the stairs and out through the front door, which she had to unlock. She did not make a single sound.

Mortimer had quieted down just a little inside the

meat safe, but he was very far from asleep. He was making a miserable mumbling, groaning sound to himself, and kicking and scratching with his claws. Arabel softly undid the catch.

"Hush, Mortimer!" she whispered. "We don't want to wake them."

They could hear Uncle Urk's snores coming out through the bedroom window. The sound was like somebody grinding a bunch of rusty wires along a section of corrugated iron, ending with a tremendous rattle.

Mortimer was so glad to see Arabel that he went quite silently. She lifted him out of the meat safe and held him tight, flattening his feathers, which were all endways and ruffled. Then she carried him back up the stairs to her bedroom.

Mortimer did not usually like sleeping on a bed; he preferred a bread bin or a coal scuttle or the

bathroom cupboard; but he had been so horrified by the meat safe that he was happy to share Arabel's eiderdown, though he did peck a hole in it so that most of the feathers came out. Either because of all the feathers flying around or because of the excitements of the day, neither Arabel nor Mortimer slept very well.

Mortimer was dreaming about giraffes. Arabel was dreaming about Noah the boa.

After an hour or so, Mortimer suddenly shot bolt upright in bed.

"What is it, Mortimer?" whispered Arabel. She knew that Mortimer's ears were very keen, like those of an owl; he could hear a potato crisp fall onto a carpeted floor half a mile away.

Mortimer turned his head, intently listening. Now even Arabel thought she could hear something, past Uncle Urk's snores—a soft series of muffled thumps.

"Oh my goodness, Mortimer! Do you think those men are stealing Lord Donisthorpe's giraffes?"

Mortimer did think so. His boot-button black eyes gleamed with pleasure at the thought. Arabel could see this because the moon was shining brightly through the window.

"I had better wake up Uncle Urk," said Arabel. "Though Aunt Effie will be cross, because she said she didn't want to hear me."

She went and tapped on Uncle Urk's door and

said in a soft, polite voice, so as not to disturb Aunt Effie, "Uncle Urk. Would you come out, please? We believe that thieves are stealing your giraffes."

But the noise made by Uncle Urk as he snored was so tremendous that neither he nor Effie (who was snoring a bit on her own account) could possibly hear Arabel's polite tones.

"Oh dear, Mortimer," said Arabel then. "I wonder what we had better do."

Mortimer plainly thought that they ought to let well enough alone. His expression suggested that if every giraffe in the zoo were hijacked, he, personally, would not raise any objection.

"Perhaps we could wake up Lord Donisthorpe," Arabel said, and she went downstairs and into the garden, with Mortimer sitting on her shoulder.

But when they were close to it, Lord Donisthorpe's castle looked very difficult to enter. There was a moat, and a drawbridge, which was raised, and a massive wooden door, which was shut.

Then Arabel remembered that Chris slept in a wooden hut near the ostrich enclosure.

"We'll wake Chris," she told Mortimer. "He'll know what to do."

Mortimer was greatly enjoying the trip through the moonlit zoo. He did not mind where they went, or what they did, as long as they did not go back to bed too soon.

Arabel walked quietly over the grass in her bedroom slippers. "Chris sleeps in the hut with red geraniums in the window boxes," she said. "He showed it to me while the doughnuts were cooking."

"Kaaark," said Mortimer, thinking about doughnuts.

Arabel walked up to the hut with the red geraniums and banged on the door.

"Chris!" she called softly. "It's me—Arabel! Will you open the door, please?"

It took a long time to wake Chris. Nobody had pumped any gas under his door; he was just naturally a very heavy sleeper. But at last he woke and came stumbling and yawning to open the door. He was very surprised to see Arabel.

"Arabel! And Mortimer! Whatever are you doing up at this time of night? Your aunt Effie would blow her top!"

"Shhh!" said Arabel. "Chris, Mortimer and I think there are thieves in the zoo. Can't you hear a kind of thumping and bumping coming from the zebra house?"

Chris listened and thought he could. "I'd best set off the alarm," he said. "Lord Donisthorpe always tells us, 'Better ten false alarms than lose one animal.'"

He pressed the alarm button, which ought to have let off tremendously loud sirens at different points all over the park, but nothing happened.

"That's funny," Chris said, scratching his head
and yawning some more. Then his eyes and his
mouth opened wide, and he said, "Blimey! It *must* be
thieves. They must have cut the wire. I'd best go on
my bike and rouse Lord Donisthorpe. I know a back
way into the castle, and then he can phone the police. *You'd* better stop here, Arabel, until I get back;
you shouldn't be running about the zoo in your slippers if there's thieves around."

Chris started off on his bike toward Lord Donisthorpe's castle. Arabel would have stayed in his hut, as he asked her, but Mortimer had other ideas. He hoisted himself off Arabel's shoulder and began flapping heavily along the ground in the direction of the giraffe house.

"Mortimer!" called Arabel. "Come back!"

But Mortimer took no notice, and so Arabel started in pursuit of him.

To Arabel's horror, as she went after Mortimer, she saw a truck parked outside the zebra house. Men with black bowler hats, crammed so far down over their heads that their faces were invisible, stood by the truck, packing in limp zebras which seemed to be fast asleep.

"Oh, how awful!" said Arabel. "Mortimer, stop! The thieves are stealing the zebras!"

But Mortimer was not interested in zebra thieves. He had only one idea in his head and that was to get to the doughnut machine near the giraffe house. The thieves did not notice Arabel and Mortimer pass by, and Arabel caught up with Mortimer just as he perched on the machine.

"Kaaark!" he said, giving the machine a hopeful kick.

"If I get you a doughnut, Mortimer, will you come back with me quietly to Chris's hut?" said Arabel.

She had the tenpenny piece that Lord Donisthorpe
had given her in her dressing-gown pocket.

Mortimer made no answer but jumped up and
down on top of the machine.

So Arabel put her coin in the slot, and Mortimer,
almost standing on his head with interest and enthusiasm, watched the doughnut slide down into the oil
to cook; then he watched the hook hoist it out and the
puffer blow white crystals all over it; then he watched
it tumble out into the paper cup; then he grabbed it,
jumped down off the machine, and disappeared in
the direction of the giraffe house.

"Mortimer, come back!" called Arabel. "You
promised—!"

But that was all she said, for the next minute she
found herself wrapped up as tightly as if twenty yards
of oil pipeline had been wound round her, and she
found herself staring, stiff with fright, straight into
the thoughtful face of Noah the boa.

4

Meanwhile the thieves, working at top speed, had packed all the drugged zebras into their truck, with layers of foam rubber in between. Then they went on to the ostriches. It was easy to drug the ostriches; all they needed to do was sprinkle chloroform on the sand where the ostriches hid their heads, and then make an alarming noise; in five minutes all the ostriches were out flat.

"D'you reckon we've time to take in a few camels as well as the giraffes?" asked Fred, the truck driver, when the ostriches were packed in. "Camels are fetching very fancy prices just now up Blackpool way."

But the short fat man was looking toward Lord Donisthorpe's castle, where a light had come on in one of the windows high up.

"That looks like trouble," he said. "Maybe the old geezer heard something. We better not fool around; go straight for the giraffes, get them packed in, and get away."

At this moment Lord Donisthorpe was speaking on the phone to the local police. "Yes, Inspector; as I just told you, we have reason to believe that there are thieves on my estate, engaged in stealing animals—*who* told me so? I understand that a raven, of unusually acute hearing, informed a young person named Arabel Jones, who informed a youthful attendant at the zoo—who informed *me*—"

At this moment also, Noah the boa, who had decided, after careful inspection of Arabel, that she looked as if she might be good to eat—probably not

quite as good as a doughnut, but still much better than a rabbit—had thrown an extra loop of himself round both Arabel and the doughnut machine, to which he was hitched, and had begun to squeeze, at the same time opening his mouth wider and wider.

But his squeezing had an unexpected effect. It started the doughnut machine working, just as if somebody had put in a coin.

Arabel, doing her best to keep quite calm, said politely, "Excuse me, but if you wouldn't mind undoing the coil that is holding my hands, *here,* I would be able to press the lever and then I could get you a doughnut, if you'd like?"

Noah was not very bright, but he did understand the word *doughnut,* and Arabel's wriggling of her hands indicated what she meant. He loosened one of his coils; Arabel pressed the lever twice; and the machine ever so quickly sugared a doughnut and tossed it out into a paper cup. Noah swallowed it in a flash and, as the machine was still working, Arabel pressed the lever again.

Meanwhile the thieves had quietly moved their truck on to the giraffe house, parked, and gone inside.

"Blimey," said Fred, "what, in the name of all that's 'orrible, 'as been going on 'ere?"

For when they shone their flashlights around, a scene of perfectly hopeless confusion was revealed: all that could be seen was legs of giraffes at the

bottom of the spiral stair, while their necks, like some dreadfully tangled piece of knitting, were all twined up inside the spiral.

"Strewth!" said the short fat man. "How are we *ever* going to get them out of there?"

Meanwhile Lord Donisthorpe and Chris, both riding bicycles, were dashing through the zoo, hunting for the malefactors. Chris was dreadfully worried about Arabel because he had found his hut empty; he kept calling, as he rode along, "Arabel? Mortimer? Where are you?"

At this moment the thieves, feverishly trying to untangle the necks of the giraffes and drag them out of the spiral stair, heard the unmistakable gulping howl of a police-car siren coming fast.

"Here, we better scram," said the fat man.

"They got cops in helicopters?" said Fred. "The sound o' that siren seems to be coming from dead overhead."

"It's the acoustics of this building, thickhead."

"Never mind where the perishing sound's *coming* from," said the pale man. "We better hop it. At least we've got the ostriches and the zebras."

They ran for their truck. But Chris, who reached it just before them, had taken the key out of the ignition. The thieves were obliged to abandon their van and escape on foot. And as they pounded toward the distant gate, something like an enormous tube traveling at thirty miles an hour caught up with them, flung a half hitch round each of them, and brought them to the ground.

It was Noah, who, having for once in his life eaten as many doughnuts as he wanted, was now prepared to do his job of burglar catching.

Chris went in search of Arabel and found her, rather pale and faint, sitting by the doughnut machine. Mortimer, looking very pleased with himself indeed, was perched on her shoulder, still giving his celebrated imitation of a police-car siren.

When the real police turned up half an hour later, all they had to do was take the thieves off to jail. Then, greatly to Arabel's relief, Lord Donisthorpe took Noah back to his cage, wheeling him in a barrow.

Chris and Lord Donisthorpe had already unpacked the ostriches and zebras and laid them out in the fresh air to sleep off the effects of the drug they had been given.

But it took ever so much longer to untangle the giraffes from the spiral stair. In fact, they were obliged to dismantle the top part of their stair altogether.

"I can't think how they ever *got* their necks in like this," said Lord Donisthorpe, panting. "Let alone *why*."

Chris thought he could guess. He had found traces of doughnut on each step all the way up.

"Perhaps it's not such a good idea to have a spiral stair in the giraffe house," murmured Lord Donisthorpe as the last captive—Wendy—was carefully pulled out, set upright on her spindly legs, and given a pail of giraffe food to revive her.

"Well, I certainly am greatly obliged to you three," added Lord Donisthorpe to Arabel and Chris, who had helped to extract Wendy, and to Mortimer, who had been sitting on the stair rail and enjoying the spectacle. "If not for you, my zoo would have suffered severe losses tonight, and I hope I can do something for you in return."

Chris said politely that he didn't think he wanted anything. He just liked working in the zoo.

Mortimer didn't even bother to reply. He was remembering how enjoyable it had been to entice

Wendy, Elsie, and Derek farther and farther up the spiral stair by holding the doughnut just in front of their noses.

But Arabel said, "Oh, please, Lord Donisthorpe. Could you please ask Aunt Effie *not* to shut Mortimer up in the meat safe? He does hate it so."

"Perhaps it would be best," said Lord Donisthorpe thoughtfully, "if Mortimer came to stay with me in my castle while you remain at Foxwell. I believe ravens are often to be found in castles. And there is really very little harm he can do there, if any."

"Oh, *yes*," said Arabel. "He'd *love* to live in a castle, wouldn't you, Mortimer?"

"Kaaark," said Mortimer.

And so that is what happened.

Aunt Effie and Uncle Urk were quite astonished when they woke up next morning and learned all that had been going on during the night. But Aunt Effie was not able to scold Arabel or Mortimer, as Lord Donisthorpe said they had been the means of saving all his ostriches and zebras, not to mention the giraffes.

Arabel soon became very fond of Wendy, Derek, and Elsie; though she had continual trouble preventing Mortimer from teasing them.

But she never did get to like Noah the boa.

Mortimer
and the
Sword Excalibur

1

It was a fine spring morning in Rainwater Crescent, Rumbury Town, north London. Arabel Jones and Mortimer, Arabel's raven, were sitting on Arabel's bedroom windowsill, which was a very wide and comfortable one, with plenty of room for both of them and a cushion as well. They were both looking out of the window, watching the work that was going on across the road in Rainwater Crescent Garden.

This garden, which was quite large, went most of the way along the inside of Rainwater Crescent, which curved round like a banana. So the garden was curved on one side and straight on the other, like a section from an enormous orange. In it there were ten trees,

quite a wide lawn, some flower beds, six benches, two statues, a sandpit for children, and a flat paved bit in the middle, where a band sometimes played.

Arabel liked spending the afternoon in Rainwater Garden, but she was not allowed to go there on her own, because of crossing the street. However, sometimes Mrs. Jones took her across and left her if Mr. Walpole, the Rumbury Town municipal gardener, was there to keep an eye on her.

Today a whole lot of interesting things were happening in the garden directly across the road from the Joneses' house.

Before breakfast a huge excavator with a long metal neck and a pair of grabbing jaws like a crocodile had come trundling along the road. And it had started in at once, very fast, digging a deep hole. This was to be the entrance to an underground parking garage, which was going to be right underneath Rainwater Crescent Garden. The excavator had dug its deep hole at the end of the garden where the children's sandpit used to be. Arabel was sorry about that; so was Mortimer. They had been fond of playing in the sandpit. Arabel liked building castles; Mortimer liked jumping on them and flattening them out. Also, he liked burrowing deep in the sand, working it in thoroughly among his feathers, and then waiting till he was home to shake himself out. But now there was a hole as deep as a house where the sandpit had been, and a lot of men standing round the edge of it, talking to one another and waving their arms in a very excited manner, while the excavator stood idly beside them, doing nothing, and hanging its head like a horse that wants its feedbag.

While the excavator had been at work digging, a large crowd of people had collected to watch it. Now that it had stopped, they had all wandered off and were doing different things in the Crescent Garden. Some were flying kites. The kites were all kinds— like boats, like birds, like fish, and some that were just long silvery streamers which very easily got caught in trees and hung there flapping. Mr. Walpole the gardener hated that sort, because they looked untidy in

the trees, and the owners were always climbing up to rescue them, and breaking branches. Other people were skipping with skipping ropes. Others were skating on skateboards along the paved bit in the middle of the lawn where the band sometimes played. This was just right for skateboards, as it sloped up slightly at each end, which gave the skaters a good start, and they were doing beautiful things, turning and gliding and whizzing and jumping up into the air, and weaving past each other very cleverly.

Arabel specially loved watching the skaters.

"Oh, please, Ma," she said to her mother, who came into the bedroom presently and started rummaging crossly about in Arabel's clothes cupboard. "Oh, please, Ma, couldn't Mortimer and I have a skateboard? I *would* like one ever so much, and so would Mortimer, wouldn't you, Mortimer?"

But Mortimer was looking out of the window very intently and did not reply.

"A *skateboard*?" said Mrs. Jones, who seemed put out about something. "In the name of goodness, what will you think of next. I should think *not,* indeed! Nasty, dangerous things, break your leg as soon as you look at them, ought to be banned by Act of Parking Lot, they should, banging into people's shins and

139

shopping baskets in the High Street. Oh my dear cats alive, *now* what am I going to do? Granny Jones has just phoned to say she'll be coming tomorrow morning, and your blue velveteen pinafore at the cleaners' because of that time Mortimer got excited with the éclairs at Penny Conway's birthday party; and I haven't yet made you a dress out of that piece of pink georgette that Granny Jones brought for you the last time she came; I'll just have to run it up into a frock for you now; why ever in the world can't Granny Jones give us a bit more *notice* before she comes on a visit, I'd like to ask? There's the best sheets at the laundry, too, oh dear, I don't know I'm sure—"

And Mrs. Jones bustled off down the stairs again.

Arabel wrapped her arms round her knees. She liked Granny Jones, but the pink georgette sounded very chilly; Arabel hated having new clothes tried on because of the drafts, and her mother's cold hands, and the pins that sometimes got stuck in her; besides, she would much rather have gone on wearing her jeans and sweater.

Mortimer the raven had taken no notice of this conversation. He was sitting as quiet as a mushroom, watching Mr. Walpole the gardener, who had gone to the shed where he kept his tools, and wheeled out an enormous grass-cutting machine called a LawnSabre.

Just now this LawnSabre was Mortimer's favorite

thing in the whole world, and he spent a lot of every day hoping that he would see Mr. Walpole using it. What Mortimer wanted even more was to be allowed to drive the LawnSabre himself. It was not at all likely that he *would* be allowed; firstly, the Lawn-Sabre was very dangerous, because it had two terribly sharp blades that whirled round and round underneath. It was covered all over with warning notices in large print: DO NOT USE THIS MACHINE UNLESS WEARING DOUBLE-THICK LEATHER BOOTS WITH METAL TOE CAPS. NEVER ALLOW THIS MACHINE NEAR CHILDREN. DO NOT RUN THIS MACHINE BACKWARDS OR SIDEWAYS OR UPHILL OR DOWNHILL. NEVER TRY TO LIFT THIS MACHINE UNTIL THE BLADES HAVE COMPLETELY STOPPED TURNING. Secondly, Mr. Walpole was very particular indeed about his machine and never let anybody else touch it, even humans, let alone ravens.

Now Mr. Walpole was starting it up. First he turned a couple of switches. Then, very energetically, he pulled out a long string half a dozen times. At about the eighth or ninth pull the machine suddenly let out a loud chattering roar. Mortimer watched all this very closely; his head was stuck forward, and his black boot-button eyes were bright with interest. Next, Mr. Walpole wheeled the LawnSabre onto the grass, keeping his booted feet well out of its way. He pulled a lever and pushed the machine off across the lawn, leaving a long stripe of neat short grass behind, like a stair carpet, as the blades underneath whirled round, shooting out a shower of cut grass blades.

"Kaaark," said Mortimer gently to himself, and he began to jump up and down.

"It's no use, Mortimer," said Arabel, who guessed what he meant. "I'm afraid Mr. Walpole would never let you push his mower."

"Nevermore," said Mortimer.

"Why don't you watch Sandy Smith?" said Arabel. "He's doing a lot of lovely things."

Mortimer sank his head into his neck feathers in a very dejected manner. He was not interested in Sandy Smith; and Mr. Walpole was now far away, over on the opposite side of the paved central area where the skaters were skating.

Arabel, however, paid careful attention to the things that Sandy Smith was doing. He was a boy who lived in Rainwater Crescent, next door but three to the Joneses, and he was training to go into a circus. He had come out into the Crescent Garden to practice his act, and he was doing tricks with three balls.

He was throwing them up into the air, one after another, and catching them with a hand under his knee, or behind his back, or in his mouth, or under his chin, or bouncing them off his knee, his elbow, his nose, the top of his head, or the sole of his foot;

meanwhile, he played a tune on a nose organ which was clipped to his nose.

Arabel thought Sandy very clever indeed, though she could not hear the tune because of the noise made by Mr. Walpole's mower. But Mortimer was still watching Mr. Walpole, who had now worked his way round to this side of the garden again.

"Arabel, dearie," called her mother. "Come down here a minute. I want to measure you before I cut out your dress. You've grown at least an inch since I made your blue."

"*You'd* better come, too, Mortimer," said Arabel.

"Nevermore," grumbled Mortimer, who would sooner have stayed on the windowsill watching Mr.

Walpole cutting the grass. But Arabel picked him up and tucked him firmly under her arm. Left to himself, Mortimer had been known to chew all the putty out from the window frame, so that the glass fell out into the front garden.

Arabel carried Mortimer down the stairs into the dining room. There, Mrs. Jones had pulled out her pedal sewing machine from where it stood by the wall and taken off the lid; and on the dining table she had laid out a long strip of pale, flimsy pink material. It looked very thin and chilly to Arabel.

"Take your cardigan off, dearie," said Mrs. Jones. "I want to measure round your middle."

Arabel put Mortimer on the windowsill. But this window looked out into the Joneses' back garden, where nothing interesting was happening. Mortimer flopped across onto a chair and began studying Mrs. Jones's sewing machine.

A sewing machine was not a LawnSabre, but it was better than nothing. At least it was *there*, right in the room.

"Kaaark," said Mortimer thoughtfully to himself.

Arabel slowly took off her nice thick, warm cardigan.

Mortimer inspected the sewing machine. It had a bobbin of pink thread on top, a big wheel at the right-hand end, a lot of silvery twiddles at the other end,

and a needle that went up and down between the metal toes of a two-pronged foot.

"Ma," said Arabel when she had been measured and put on her cardigan again—the cardigan felt cold now—"Ma, couldn't you take Mortimer and me across the road into the Crescent Garden? Sandy's there, juggling, and Mr. Walpole, too; he'd keep an eye on us—"

"No time just now," said Mrs. Jones through one corner of her mouth—the rest of her mouth was pressed tight on a row of pins—"besides, I'll be wanting to measure again in a minute. Why can't you play in the back garden, nicely, with your spade and fork?"

"Because we want to watch Sandy and Mr. Walpole," said Arabel.

"Kaaark," said Mortimer. He wanted to watch the LawnSabre.

"Well, if you want to watch, you'd better go back upstairs," said Mrs. Jones. "I'll need you again as soon as I've sewed up the skirt."

She laid a piece of paper pattern over the pink stuff on the table, pinned it on with some of the pins from her mouth, and started quickly snipping round the edge. The scissors made a gritty, scrunching noise along the table; every now and then Mrs. Jones stopped to make a snick in the edge of the pink stuff. Then, when she had two large fan-shaped pieces cut out, she unpinned the paper pattern from them, pinned them to each other, and slid them under the metal foot of the sewing machine.

"What are those pieces?" asked Arabel.

"That's the back and front of the skirt," said Mrs. Jones, sitting down at the sewing machine and starting to work the pedal with her foot.

Mortimer could not see this from where he sat. But he saw the bobbin of pink thread on top of the machine suddenly start to spin round. The big wheel turned, and the needle flashed up and down. The pieces of pink skirt suddenly shot backward onto the floor.

"Kaark," said Mortimer, much interested.

"Drat!" said Mrs. Jones. "Left the machine in reverse. That's what comes of answering questions. Do run along, Arabel dear; and take Mortimer with you.

It always makes me nervous when he's in the room; I'm always expecting him to do something horrible."

Arabel picked up Mortimer (who had indeed begun to sidle toward Mrs. Jones's biscuit tin full of red and brown and pink and blue and green and white and yellow spools of thread, after studying them in a very thoughtful manner). She carried him upstairs and put him back on her bedroom windowsill.

Across the road, in Rainwater Crescent Garden, the big excavator was still idly hanging its head, while the group of men still stood on the edge of the huge crater it had dug, arguing and waving their hands about. Sometimes one or another of them would climb down a ladder and vanish into the hole.

"Perhaps they've found a dinosaur down there," said Arabel. "I do wish we could see to the bottom of the hole."

But the hole was too deep for that. From where they sat, they could see only a bit of the side.

Mr. Walpole, pushing the LawnSabre, had now cut a wide circle of grass all round the paved middle section. And Sandy the juggler had put away his three balls. Instead, he had lit three flaming torches, which he was tossing into the air and catching just as easily as if they were not shooting out plumes of red and yellow fire.

"*Coo,* Mortimer," said Arabel. "Look at that!"

"Kaaark," said Mortimer. But he was really much more interested in following the course of Mr. Walpole and the LawnSabre. He was remembering a plane that he had once seen take off at Heathrow Airport when the family went to say good-bye to Aunt Flossie from Toronto; and he was hoping that Mr. Walpole and the LawnSabre would presently take right off into the air.

Now Sandy the juggler stuck his three torches into a patch of loose earth, where they continued to burn. He pulled a long piece of rope out of his bag, which lay beside him on the ground. Looking round, he saw a plane tree that grew on a piece of lawn already mowed by Mr. Walpole. Sandy ran to this tree, climbed up it like a squirrel, tied one end of his rope quite high up its trunk, and jumped down again. Then, going to a second tree that grew about twenty feet from the first, he climbed up and tied the other end of the rope to *that* tree.

"He's put up a clothesline," said Arabel, poking Mortimer. "That's funny! Do you think he's going to hang up some laundry, Mortimer?"

"Kaaark," said Mortimer, not paying much attention. He had his eye on Mr. Walpole and the Lawn-Sabre.

But now Sandy climbed back up the first tree, carrying two of his three torches in his teeth. And then he began to walk very slowly along the rope, holding on to it with his toes and balancing himself with his arms spread out. In each hand was a flaming torch.

"*Look*, Mortimer," said Arabel. "He's walking on the *rope!*"

Mortimer *was* quite amazed at that. He looked at Sandy balancing on the rope, and muttered, "Nevermore," to himself.

"Bet *you* couldn't do that, Mortimer," said Arabel.

However, at this moment Sandy dropped one of his torches, and Mr. Walpole shouted, "'Ere, you! Don't you singe my turf, young feller, or I'll singe *you*, good and proper!"

So Sandy jumped down again, put away his torches, and went up with a long rod instead. Holding each end of this with his hands stretched out wide apart, he began slowly walking along the rope once more.

"Arabel dearie, will you come downstairs?" called Mrs. Jones. "I've sewn up the skirt, and I want to try it on you for length."

"Oh, please, Ma," said Arabel, "I want to watch

Sandy. He's doing ever such interesting things. He's walking along the rope. Must I come just now?"

"Yes, you must!" called Mrs. Jones sharply. "I've a lot to do and I haven't got all day. Come along down at once and bring that feathered wretch with you, else he'll get up to mischief if he's left alone."

Arabel picked up Mortimer and went slowly downstairs again.

Mrs. Jones wrapped the pink skirt round Arabel, over her jeans, and then led her out into the front hall, where there was a long mirror.

"Stand still and don't wriggle while I pin it up," she said, with her mouth full of pins. "Stand up

straight, Arabel, can't you? I want to pin the hem and I can't if you keep leaning over sideways."

Arabel was trying to see what Mortimer was doing; she had left him on the dining-room table.

"Mortimer?" she called.

But while Mrs. Jones was pinning up the skirt hem, Mortimer was carefully studying all the pieces of pink material on the table. He swallowed a good many of them. Then, deciding that they did not taste interesting, he flopped quickly across from the table to Mrs. Jones's sewing machine. Remembering the way that Mr. Walpole started the LawnSabre by pulling a string, he tried to start the sewing machine by giving a tremendous tug to the pink thread that dangled down through the eye of the needle.

Nothing happened, except that he undid a whole lot of thread and the bobbin whirled round and round.

Soon there was a thick tangle of thread, like a swan's nest, all round the sewing machine, as Mortimer tugged and tugged. But still the machine would not start.

"Nevermore," uttered Mortimer irritably.

At last, after he had given a particularly vigorous tug, the needle broke off and the bottom half came sliding down the thread on its eye. So then Mortimer swallowed the needle.

Giving up on the thread, he then tried pushing round the big wheel with his claw. Then he tried unscrewing a knob on top of the machine. Nothing happened, so he swallowed the knob. Then he pushed up a metal flap, under where the needle had been, and stuck his beak into the hole under the flap. The beak would not go in very far, so he poked in his claw, which came out with a shiny metal spindle on it; so Mortimer swallowed this, too. But as he *still* had not managed to start the sewing machine, he finally gave it up in disgust, flopped down onto the floor, and walked off into the front hall just as Mrs. Jones finished pinning the hem of Arabel's skirt.

"*That's* done, then," said Mrs. Jones. "I'll hem it up this afternoon. Now we'd better have a bite to eat or that bird will get up to mischief; he always does when he's hungry. Shut the dining-room door, Arabel, so he can't get in; you can hang your skirt over the ironing board in the kitchen."

Arabel, Mortimer, and Mrs. Jones had their lunch in the kitchen. Mrs. Jones and Arabel had tomato soup and battered fish fingers. Mortimer did not care for soup; he just had the fish fingers, and he battered his even more by throwing them into the air, chopping them in half with his beak as they came down, and then jumping on them to make them really squashy.

After that they had bananas.

Mortimer unpeeled his banana by pecking the peel at the stalk end, and then, firmly holding on to

the stalk, he whirled the banana round and round his head like a sling thrower.

"*Mortimer!* You must go outside if you want to do that!" said Mrs. Jones, but she said it just too late. Mortimer's banana shot out of its skin and flew through the air; it became stuck among the bristles of the stiff broom which was leaning upside down against the kitchen wall. Mrs. Jones was very annoyed about this, but not nearly so annoyed as Mortimer, who had a very difficult time picking bits of banana out from among the broom bristles.

Mrs. Jones refused to give him another.

"When three bananas cost forty pence?" she said. "Are you joking? He must just make do with what he can get out."

When they had washed up the lunch dishes and Mrs. Jones went back into the dining room and discovered what Mortimer had been doing, there was a fearful scene.

"Just wait till I get my hands on that blessed bird!" shrieked Mrs. Jones. "I'll put him in the dustbin and shut the lid on him! I'll scour him with a Scrubbo pad! I'll spray him with oven spray!"

"Kaaark," said Mortimer, who was sitting on the dining-room mantelpiece.

"I'll kaaark you, my boy. I'll make you kaaark on the other side of your face!"

However, Mrs. Jones was really in too much of a hurry to finish making Arabel's dress and tidy the house before the arrival of Granny Jones to carry out any of her threats.

She cut off the tangle of pink thread and threw it all away; she put a new needle and spindle onto the machine, replaced the knob on top from her box of spare parts, set the needle to hem, and put Arabel's skirt under the foot. Then she started to sew.

Mrs. Jones's sewing machine was not new; and Mortimer's treatment had upset it; it began doing terrible things. It stuck fast with a loud grinding noise, it puckered up the pink material, it refused to sew at all, or poured out great handfuls of thread, and then sewed in enormously wide stitches, which hardly held the cloth together.

"*Drat* that Mortimer," muttered Mrs. Jones, furiously putting Arabel's pink waistband under the foot to sew it for the third time, after she had ripped out all the loose stitching. "I wish he was at the bottom of the sea, that I do!"

Suddenly the machine began sewing all by itself, very fast, before Mrs. Jones was ready for it.

"*Now* what's the matter with it?" cried Mrs. Jones. "Has it gone bewitched?"

"Mortimer's on the pedal, Ma," said Arabel.

Mortimer had at last discovered what made the machine go. He was sitting on the foot pedal and making the needle race very fast, in a zigzag course, along the pink waistband.

"*Get* off there!" said Mrs. Jones, and she would have removed Mortimer from the pedal with her foot if he had not removed himself very speedily and gone back to the mantelpiece.

"Ma, couldn't Mortimer and I go into Rainwater Garden now?" said Arabel. "You've done the trying on, and you needn't come across the road with us; you could just watch to see we go when there's no traffic. And Mr. Walpole's there; he'd keep an eye on us. And Sandy's still there doing tricks. And you know you sew ever so much better when Mortimer isn't around."

"I could sew ever so much better if he wasn't in the *world*," said Mrs. Jones. "Oh, very well! Put on your parka, then. Anything to get that black monster out from under my feet."

So Arabel ran joyfully to get her parka and her skipping rope, while Mortimer jumped up and down a great many times, shouting, "Nevermore!" with great enthusiasm and satisfaction.

Then Mrs. Jones watched them safely across the road and through the gate into Rainwater Garden.

"Don't you go far from the gate, now!" she called. "And don't you get near that Bullroarer, Arabel! I don't want you chopped up, or squashed flat, or falling down that big hole it's dug."

"What about Mortimer?"

"I don't care *what* happens to him," said Mrs. Jones.

2

Just inside the gate of Rainwater Crescent Garden Mr. Walpole the gardener was standing, talking to a bald man.

"Hullo, Mr. Walpole," said Arabel, running up to him. "Ma says that Mortimer and me are to be in your charge."

"That's all right, dearie," said Mr. Walpole absently, listening to what the bald man was saying to him. "I'll keep an eye on ye. Just don't ye goo near my LawnSabre, that's all... Is that so, then, Mr. Dunnage, about the hole? That'll put a stop to that-thurr municipal car-park plan, then, I dessay?"

"It certainly will, till we can get someone from

158

the British Museum to come and have a look," said
Mr. Dunnage, who taught history at Rumbury Com-
prehensive, and was also on the Rumbury Historical
Preservation Society, and he hurried off to Rumbury
underground station to fetch a friend of his from the
British Museum.

"Seems they found su'thing val'ble down in that-
urr dratted great hole they bin an' dug just whurr my
compost heap used to be," said Mr. Walpole. "*I*
could'a' told 'em! I allus said 'twould be a mistake to
go a-digging in Rainwater Gardens. Stands to reason,

if there'd a bin meant to be a car-park under thurr, thurr wouldn't a-bin a garden 'ere, dunnit?"

"What did they find down in the hole, Mr. Walpole?" said Arabel.

"*I* dunno," said Mr. Walpole. "Mr. Dunnage, 'e said they found su'think that sounded like a sort o' 'sparagus. But *that* can't be right. For one thing, I ain't put *in* no 'sparagus, ner likely to, and second, 'sparagus ain't a root vegetable, let alone you'd never find it down so deep as that."

And he stumped away, whistling all on one note, to his LawnSabre, which was standing near the paved part in the middle of the garden.

Mortimer instantly started walking after Mr. Walpole with such a meaningful expression that Arabel said quickly: "Come on, Mortimer, let's see if we can find out what the valuable thing is at the bottom of the deep hole. Maybe it's treasure!"

And she picked up Mortimer and carried him in the other direction.

"Kaaark," said Mortimer, twisting his head round disappointedly.

But when they reached the edge of the enormous hole, even Mortimer was so interested that, for a time, he almost forgot about the LawnSabre. The hole was so deep that a guardrail had been rigged up round the edge and a series of ladders led down to the bottom. Standing by the rail and looking over, Arabel and Mortimer could just see down as far as the bottom, where about a dozen people were craning and pushing to look at something in the middle.

"What have they found down there?" Arabel asked a boy with a skateboard, who was standing beside her.

"Somebody said it was a round table," said the boy.

"A *table*? *That* doesn't sound very valuable," said Arabel, disappointed. "I thought they'd found something like a king's crown. Why should a table be valuable? Why should a table be down at the bottom of a hole?"

"*I* dunno," said the boy. "Maybe it's a vegy-table! Ha, ha, ha!" And he stepped onto his skateboard, pushed off, and glided away down the path. Arabel gazed after him with envy. But Mortimer, staring down into the great crater, was struggling and straining in Arabel's arms. He wanted to go down the ladder and see for himself what was at the bottom.

"*No*, Mortimer," said Arabel. "*You* can't go down there. How would you get back? You'd have to fly, and you know you don't like that. Come and see what Sandy's doing. He's got his fiery torches again."

She carried the unwilling Mortimer back to the circle of watchers round Sandy Smith, who was now swallowing great gulps of fire from his blazing torches and then spitting them out again.

"Coo, he *is* clever," said Arabel. "How would you like to do that, Mortimer?"

"Nevermore," muttered Mortimer.

He would swallow almost *any*thing so long as it was hard; but fire always made him nervous, and he edged backward when Sandy blew out a mouthful of flame.

Then Sandy stuck his fiery torches into the loose earth of a flower bed and pulled a wheel out of his bag. The wheel was a bit bigger than an LP disk, and it had a pedal on each side. Sandy put his feet on the pedals, and suddenly—*whizz*—he began to cycle

round and round inside the ring of people who were watching. He made it look very easy by sticking his hands into his pockets and playing a tune on his nose organ as he pedaled along. Then he began to go faster and faster, leaning inward on the bends like a tree blown by the wind. Everybody clapped like mad, and Mortimer jumped up and down. He had wriggled out of Arabel's arms and was standing on the ground beside her.

Then Sandy noticed Arabel standing among the watchers.

"Hi, Arabel," he said, "like a ride on my shoulders?"

"*Could* I?" said Arabel.

"Why not?" said Sandy. "Come on!" He stepped off his wheel—which at once fell over on its side—picked up Arabel, and perched her on his shoulders, with a foot dangling forward on each side of his face.

"Hold on tight!" he said.

"*Kaaark!*" shouted Mortimer, who did not want to be left behind.

But Sandy, who had not noticed Mortimer, got back onto his wheel and began riding round and round in a circle again. Arabel felt as if she were flying; the wind rushed past her face, and when he went round a tight curve Sandy leaned over so far that there was nothing between her and the ground.

"Oh, it's lovely!" cried Arabel. "Mortimer! Look at me, Mortimer!"

But Mortimer was not looking at Arabel. Very annoyed at being left behind, he had turned his black head right round on its neck and was looking for Mr. Walpole and the LawnSabre. Then he started walking purposefully away from the group of people who were watching Sandy.

"Sandy," said Arabel as he whizzed round and round, "why are they getting someone from the British Museum to look at the thing they found in that hole if it's only a table?"

Arabel thought Sandy must know all about it, as he had been in the garden since breakfast time, and sure enough he did.

"They found a great big round, flat stone thing," he said, pedaling away. "It's just about as big as this circle I'm making."

He did another whirl round, and Arabel, who was getting a little giddy, clutched hold of his hair with both hands. Luckily there was plenty of hair to hold on to, bright ginger in color.

"Why should a man from the British Museum come to look at a big round stone thing?"

"Because they think it's King Arthur's Round Table, that's why!"

Sandy shot off down a path, did a circle round two trees, and came back the same way that he had gone.

"What makes them think that?" asked Arabel, holding on even tighter, and ducking her head, as they passed under some trees with low branches.

"Because there's a long sword stuck right in the middle of the stone table. And it has a red sparkling ruby in the handle. And they think it might be King Arthur's sword Excalibur!"

Arabel had never heard of King Arthur's sword Excalibur, and she was beginning to feel rather queer. The tomato soup, the battered fish fingers, and the banana that she had eaten for her lunch had all been whizzed round inside her until her stomach felt like a spin dryer full of mixed laundry.

"I think I'd better get down now, Sandy," she said politely. "Thank you very much for the ride, but I'd better see what Mortimer is doing."

"Okay," said Sandy, and he glided to a stop beside a tree, holding his arm round the trunk as he came up to it. Then he lifted Arabel off his shoulders and put her down on the ground. Arabel found that her legs would not hold her up, and she sat down, quite suddenly, on the grass. Her head still seemed to be whirling round even though she was sitting still.

"I do feel funny," she said.

"You'll be better in a minute," said Sandy, who was used to the feeling.

Arabel tried to look around her for Mortimer, but all the trees and people and grass and daffodils seemed to be swinging round in a circle, and she had to shut her eyes.

"Can you see Mortimer anywhere, Sandy?" she asked, with her eyes shut.

But Sandy had got back onto his wheel and pedaled away; he was juggling with his three balls as he rode.

Meanwhile, where *was* Mortimer?

He was still walking slowly and purposefully toward the LawnSabre, which Mr. Walpole had left

parked just beside the little hut in the middle of the garden where he kept his tools.

In order to reach the LawnSabre, Mortimer had to cross the paved area where the skaters were gliding about on their skateboards.

"Watch out!" yelled a boy, whizzing past Mortimer on one wheel. Mortimer jumped backward, and two other skaters nearly collided as they tried to avoid him. Three more skaters shot off the pavement and ended up in a bed of daffodils.

"You mind out for my daffs, or I'll report ye to the

Borough!" bawled old Mr. Walpole angrily. He had been walking toward the toolshed to put away the LawnSabre, but now he stepped into the flower bed and began indignantly straightening up the bent daffodils and tying them to sticks, shaking his fist at the skaters.

Mortimer, taking no notice of what was happening behind him, stepped off the pavement and walked on to where the LawnSabre was standing.

The LawnSabre was bright red. It was mounted on four smallish wheels, and it had a pair of long handles, like a wheelbarrow, and a switch for the fuel, and a lever to raise or lower the blades (so as to cut the grass long or short). At present, the lever was lowered so that the blades would cut the grass as short as possible.

The motor had to be started by pulling a string, as Mortimer already knew from watching Mr. Walpole through the window.

The switch for the fuel was already switched to the ON position. Mr. Walpole had left it that way when he went off to talk to Mr. Dunnage.

Meanwhile, Arabel was beginning to feel a little better, and she was able to open her eyes. She looked around her for Mortimer, but could not see him anywhere. She stood up, holding on to a tree to balance herself, because the ground still seemed to be rocking about under her feet. She could see Sandy in the distance; he was now pedaling about, holding an open umbrella in one hand and a top hat in the other; he waved the top hat to Arabel and then put it on his head.

"Sandy, have you seen Mortimer?" called Arabel, but Sandy did not hear her.

"Are you feeling all right, my dear?" said a lady in a blue hat, walking up to Arabel. "You look rather green."

"Yes, thank you, I'm all right," said Arabel politely. "But I am anxious about my raven, Mortimer. I would like to find him. Have you seen him, please?"

"Your raven?" said the lady. "I'm afraid, my dear, that you are still a little bit dizzy. You had better sit by me quietly on this seat for a while. Then

we will look for your mummy. I am rather surprised that she let you do that dangerous ride on that boy's shoulders."

The lady obliged Arabel to sit beside her on a bench; she held on to Arabel's hand very tightly.

"Now tell me, my dear," she said, looking round the garden, "what sort of clothes is your mummy wearing? Is she a tall lady or a short one? Does she have a hat and coat on?"

"She has an overall covered with flowers," said Arabel. "But—"

Taking no notice of Arabel, the lady began stopping people as they passed by, and saying: "This little girl seems to have lost her mummy. Will you tell her, if you see her, that I have her child and am sitting on this bench?"

"Excuse me," said Arabel politely. "It isn't my mother that I have lost, but my raven, Mortimer. He doesn't have a coat, but he is quite tall for a raven. And he is black all over and has hair on his beak."

"Oh dear," said the lady, "I am afraid you are still feeling unwell, my poor child. Perhaps we had better look for a nice, kind policeman. I am sure *he* will be able to take you to your mummy, who must be very worried, wondering where you have got to."

By this time Mortimer had climbed up on top of the LawnSabre, and had found the string that was

used to start the motor. He took firm hold of it in his
strong, hairy beak.

Mr. Walpole was still crossly propping up his battered daffodils and tying them to sticks with bits of
raffia which he took out of his trouser pocket. He did
not notice what Mortimer was doing.

"Are you feeling a little better now, my dear?"
said the lady in the blue hat.

"Yes, thank you," said Arabel, at last managing
to wriggle loose from the lady's grasp. And she
climbed down from the bench.

"Then," said the lady, grabbing Arabel's hand
again, "we will go and find a nice, kind policeman."

"But I don't want a policeman," said Arabel. "I want my raven, Mortimer."

Just at that moment Mortimer gave the cord of the LawnSabre a tremendous jerk. The motor, which was still warm, burst at once into an earsplitting roar.

"Kaaark!" shouted Mortimer joyfully.

"Hey!" shouted old Mr. Walpole, looking round from his broken daffodils. "Who the pest has started my mower? Hey, you! You get away from that-urr machine. Don't you dare start it!"

But it was too late. Mortimer jumped from the starting string to the right handle of the LawnSabre. There was a switch on the handle which had four different positions: START, SLOW, FAST, and VERY FAST. Mortimer's jump shifted the switch from the START to the FAST position, and the mower began rolling over the grass.

"Oh my goodness!" said Arabel. "*There's* Mortimer!"

And, pulling her hand out of the lady's clasp, she began running toward Mortimer and the LawnSabre as fast as she could go. The LawnSabre, at the same time, was rolling equally fast toward Arabel.

"NEVERMORE!" yelled Mortimer, mad with excitement, jumping up and down on the handle of the mower. His jumping moved the lever into the VERY FAST position, and the LawnSabre began to go almost

as quickly as Sandy on his wheel, or the skaters on
their skateboards, careering across the grass toward
Arabel.

"You there! You stop that mower directly, do you
hear me?" shouted Mr. Walpole.

But Mortimer did *not* hear Mr. Walpole—the
LawnSabre was making far too much noise for him to
be able to hear anything else at all. Even if Mortimer
had heard Mr. Walpole, he would not have paid the
least attention to him. Mortimer was having a won-
derful time. The LawnSabre crashed through a bed
of daffodils and tulips, mowing them as flat as a
bath mat.

Mr. Walpole let out a bellow of rage. "Stop that, you black monster!" he shouted. "You bring that-urr mower back here!"

But Mortimer did not have the least intention of stopping the LawnSabre. And, even if he had meant to, he did not know how to stop the motor.

The LawnSabre went on racing across a stretch of grass which had already been cut once, and then it crossed the paved strip where the skaters were skating. The noise made by the metal blades on the stone pavement was dreadful—like a giant mincer grinding up a trainload of rocks.

"Oh, my blades!" moaned Mr. Walpole, putting his hands over his ears.

Now Mortimer noticed Arabel running toward him.

With a loud shriek of pride and enjoyment, he drove the LawnSabre straight in her direction.

"WATCH OUT!" everybody shouted in horror. Mr. Walpole turned as white as one of his own snowdrops and shut his eyes. The kind lady in the blue hat fainted dead away into a bed of pink tulips. For it seemed certain that the LawnSabre would run over Arabel and mow her as flat as the daffodils.

But just then, luckily, Sandy, who had seen what was happening from the other side of the garden, came pedaling over the grass at frantic speed on his wheel. He swung round in a swooping curve and just

managed to catch up Arabel in his umbrella and whisk her out of the way of the LawnSabre as it chewed its way along.

"Oh, WELL DONE!" everybody shouted.

Mr. Walpole opened his eyes again.

Sandy and Arabel had crashed into a lilac bush, all tangled up with each other and the wheel and the umbrella, but they were not hurt. As soon as Arabel had managed to scramble out of the bush, she went running after Mortimer and the LawnSabre.

"Stop him, oh please stop him!" she panted. "Can't somebody stop him? Please! It's Mortimer, my raven!"

"All very well to say stop him, but how's a body

a-going to set about that?" demanded Mr. Walpole. "That-urr mower's still got half a tank o' fuel in her; her'll run for a good half hour yet, and dear knows where that feathered fiend'll get to in that time; he could mow his way across half London and flatten the Houses o' Parliament 'afore anybody could lay a-holt of him. What we need is a helicopter, and a grappling iron, and a posse o' motorcycle cops."

But before any of these things could be fetched, it became plain that the headlong course of the LawnSabre was likely to end in a very sudden and drastic manner. For Mortimer and the mower were now whizzing at breakneck speed straight for the

huge crater at the bottom of which the round stone
table with the sword in it had been discovered.

"Nevermore!" shouted Mortimer, looking ahead
joyfully, and remembering the jet plane he had seen
take off into the air at Heathrow Airport.

Arabel, running after him across the grass, was
now much too far behind to have any hope of catching up.

"Mortimer!" she panted. "Please turn around.
Please come back! Can't you stop the motor?"

But Mortimer could not hear her and, anyway, he
did not wish to turn or stop. With a final burst of
speed, the LawnSabre shot clean over the edge of the
huge hole, bursting through the guard fence as if it
had been made of soapsuds.

A scream of horror went up from all the people in

the garden. And the people who were down in the bottom of the hole suddenly saw a large red motor mower in midair right over their heads, with Mortimer sitting on it.

Luckily there was just time for them to jump back against the sides of the hole.

Then the LawnSabre struck the stone table at the bottom of the hole. There was a tremendous crash; the sound was so loud that it could be heard all over Rumbury Town, from the cricket ground to the pumping station.

The LawnSabre was smashed to smithereens. The round stone table was crushed to powdery rubble.

But Mortimer, discovering with great disgust that the LawnSabre was not going to take off into the air as he had expected it would, had spread his wings at the last moment and rose up into the air himself. He did not like flying, but there were times when he had to, and this was one of them.

So all the people up above in Rainwater Crescent Garden, who had rushed to the side of the hole in the expectation of seeing some dreadful calamity, were amazed to see a large black bird come flapping slowly up out of the crater, carrying a massive metal blade with a red flashing stone in the handle at one end.

As he rose up, Mortimer had grabbed at the hilt of the sword which had been stuck in the stone table; and he took it with him in his flight.

"Oh, if only I had brought my camera!" lamented Dick Otter, a young man from the *Rumbury Borough News*, who had come along because there was a rumor that King Arthur and all his knights had turned up in Rainwater Crescent.

Mortimer was feeling very ruffled. He wanted his tea. Also, he did not quite know what to do with the metal blade he had brought up with him out of the hole. It was very heavy and tasted disagreeably of old lettuce leaves left to soak too long in vinegar. Mortimer hated the feel of it in his beak. But he did like the red sparkling stone in the handle. He wanted to show it to Arabel.

Just at that moment Mr. Dunnage, the history teacher, came rushing back with a white-bearded man, who was his friend, Professor Lloyd-Williams, from the British Museum, an expert in Arthurian history.

The first thing they saw as they ran into Rainwater Crescent Garden was an openmouthed, gaping crowd, all gazing up at a rope that was stretched like a clothesline between two plane trees.

And on this rope a large black bird was walking slowly along, swaying a good deal from side to side. In his beak he held a long, heavy-looking, rusty sword with a red stone in its hilt.

"Oh dear," said Mr. Dunnage. "That looks like the sword that was stuck in the table. But how in the world did that bird get hold of it?"

"Well now, indeed," said Professor Lloyd-Williams, "that certainly does look like the sword Excalibur; for a bardic description says that it was 'longer than three men's arms, with a three-edged blade, and three red rubies in the hilt.'"

"There's only one red stone," pointed out Mr. Dunnage.

"The others might have fallen out," said the professor. "And the bird, no doubt, is one of the Ravens of Owain, who were supposed to have set upon King Arthur's warriors in battle—"

"How the deuce are we going to get the sword *away* from the bird?" said Mr. Dunnage.

Dick Otter, coming up to the two men, said, "Oh, sir, if the sword really is King Arthur's sword Excalibur, can you say what it would be worth?"

"How can I tell?" said Professor Lloyd-Williams. "It is unique. Perhaps a hundred thousand pounds. Perhaps a million."

At this moment Arabel discovered where Mortimer had got to and, standing by one of the plane trees to which the rope was tied, she called, "Mortimer! Mortimer? Please, I think you had better come down from there!"

By now Mortimer had walked about halfway across the rope, but he wasn't as good at balancing as Sandy, and he had been swaying about quite a lot. Arabel's voice distracted him, and he now toppled

right off the rope, letting go of the sword, which fell point downward, stuck into the ground, and broke into four pieces.

A terrible wail went up from the professor and Mr. Dunnage.

"Oh! The sword Excalibur!" They rushed forward to rescue the bits of sword.

Mortimer hoisted himself irritably up from the grass, and looked round for Arabel. In the general excitement over the broken sword, she was able to pick him up and carry him off toward the garden gate.

"I think perhaps we'd better go home, Mortimer," she said. "Perhaps we can get a policeman to see us across the road."

However, just as they reached the entrance, they saw her father, Mr. Jones, who had taken an hour off from taxi driving to come home for his tea.

"Hello, Arabel dearie," he said. "Your ma's sent me to fetch you. And you'd best be ever such a good quiet girl at tea—and Mortimer, too, if he *can*—because she's terribly put out."

"Why is Ma put out, Pa?" asked Arabel, as they crossed the pavement and went through their front gate.

"Because Granny Jones phoned to say she's got a sore throat and she's not coming after all. Seems your ma had just finished making you a pink dress."

Arabel was sorry that Granny Jones was not coming, but very glad that she did not have to wear the pink dress.

"It's lucky Ma doesn't know about your driving the LawnSabre, Mortimer," she said, as she went up to the bathroom to wash her hands before tea. "I don't think she'd have liked that."

"Kaaark," said Mortimer, who had almost forgotten about the LawnSabre, and was thinking about jam tarts, hoping very much there would be some for tea. He lifted one of his wings, which felt fidgety, and shook it. Out from under his wing fell the red shining stone from the hilt of King Arthur's sword. It dropped into the washbasin, rolled around with the soapy water, and went down the plughole.